YAP

ALSO AVAILABLE FROM ALAN SUTTON

Ole Biskit
by Jan Stewer

ENGLISH COUNTRY TALES

YAP

Jan Stewer

ALAN SUTTON
1987

ALAN SUTTON PUBLISHING
BRUNSWICK ROAD · GLOUCESTER

First published 1931

This paperback edition published 1987
by arrangement with the copyright holders

British Library Cataloguing in Publication Data

Stewer, Jan
Yap.
Rn: Albert John Coles   I. Title
823'.912 [F]   PR6037.T47/

ISBN 0-86299-431-4

Cover: portrait photograph of Jan Stewer

Typesetting and origination by
Alan Sutton Publishing Limited
Printed in Great Britain by
The Guernsey Press Company Limited
Guernsey, Channel Islands

CONTENTS

PAGE

THE SINGING MATCH   1

    1.   The Anthem
    2.   The Committee
    3.   Hail, Smiling Morn

THE LIKENESS TAKER   18

THE WORKING MODEL   27

JAN PLAYS GOLF   38

    1.   Seeing how it is done
    2.   Showing how to do it

GINGER'S FORTUNE   52

MRS. SNELL'S RIDE   60

THE WEDDING   66

    1.   Jan gets out of the way
    2.   The Trousseau
    3.   In proper style

LIAS IN TOWN   84

A PECK O' CIDER   91

JAN BUILDS A HOUSE   97

    1.   The plans
    2.   The finished article

THE MAN WHO LOST HIS MEMORY   108

    1.   Alfy Dispin's brain-wave

CONTENTS

2. Jim Davey takes a hand
3. After the Dance
4. Alfy comes home

JUDGMENT   131

FOR THE GOOD OF THE CAUSE   136
1. *Bal Masque*
2. King for a night

Yap is the expressive term commonly applied in rural Devon to Much Talk, particularly much talk of a trivial or frivolous character; hence its aptness as a title for this book.

THE SINGING MATCH

1. THE ANTHEM

Pitt Wollidge and Stoke Arrish is a-joining parishes, and there's alwis bin a tremenjis amount o' jellisness between 'em ever since I can mind. And longer agone than that, 'cus I've yeard the old volk say it was zac'ly zame when they was young. Anything that was done in Pitt mus' be all wrong accordin' to Stoke, and if Stoke done aught, Pitt cud'n zay nothin' bad nuff about it. I never knowed two places so jellis o' one-tother.

Didn't matter if 'twas a conzert or a dance or sports or a feet, whatever one village got up the other wude try to best it. If it rained cats and dogs for the Stoke Show, Pitt wude be jis' delighted; and if Pitt lost the vootball or got bate in the tug-o'-war that was vine job for Stoke. They didn't matter who bate 'em, so-long as zomebody did.

But the zingin' match topped the lot.

To get right to the bottom o' the zingin' match you'd have to go back, a tidy way; right back to the time when the church choir zinged a antum to Pitt. That was what you might railly call the beginnin' o' the trouble.

Previous to that there had'n bin a antum zinged into Pitt Church for zixty year. It mus' be all that, 'cus ole Georgie Lomas have played the orgin there for thirty year to my knowledge, and before that Tammas Gudeman, Will Dicker and Napper Sage played the heems on the baze vile, clar'net and viddle, when orgins and sitch-like new-vangled inventions had'n bin thought about. And there wad'n no antums zinged in their time. I know that's the case, 'cus I've yeard old Napper zay zo scores o' times. He's the only one left o' the dree musickers, and he's in his ninety-vive, zo he ought to know.

'The nearest us ever got to a antum,' ole Napper told me hiszelf, 'was when the old Squire's darter was married. I mean the real Squire, gran'vather to the present one. I'm gwain back now to the

1

year 'ighteen hunderd and vifty-zix or thereabouts, and us had news o' the finish o' the Russian war, jist about the zame time. So 'twas considered us ought to knack the two things into one, and play zummat a bit speshul. But nobody cude'n agree what us ought to play. Zome wanted, "God Zave the Quane," and zome was for, "Zee the Conquerin' Hero Comes," and others said it ought to be "Weddin' March." '

'And which one did 'ee play, Napper?' I axed 'en.

The ole feller screwed up his eyes and lookid to me for ever so long. 'You'd like for me to tell 'ee, wude'n 'ee?' he says. 'And there's plenty more have wanted me to tell 'em for the last vifty years. But I shan't. Everybody in church was satisfied with the chune us was playin', 'cus they all though they was havin' the one they wanted. There was argiments in this parish over the matter for a gineration. I've knowed it come to blows manys-a-times, and I've bin offered gallons o' beer, fust and last, if I wude tell 'em which chune it was us played. But I never told 'em, and Wi'yum Dicker never told 'em, and Tammas Gudeman never told 'em, and consequently they never knowed for certin; and so they cude never accuse us for playin' the wrong chune.'

If you was to say to ole Napper, 'Did you knaw what chune you was playin' yerzells, Napper?' he'd answer 'ee:

'I knowed what chune I was playin'. Let Tammas Gudeman and Wi'yum dicker answer vor theirzel's.'

And that's the utmost ever you'd get out of 'n.

Be that as it may, it caused such upstore in the parish 'twas never ventured on again. If anybody suggested a antum, our ole paasen use to zay:

'Let sleepin' dogs lie. Us have had one ole fol-de-dol-diddle chune in the church and nearly brought distruction on the parish. Twude be timtation of providence to have another.'

But in time as had a new paasen, a youngish feller, more up to date, like. A proper zingin' toad he was. Zinged every mortle thing, he did. He cude'n zay, "Let us Pray," without puttin' a chune to it. So he soon started to furbish up the choir. If he thought you had a zingin' face he wude'n give 'ee no rest till he'd made 'ee join, and I've many's-a-times zee'd more volks in the zingin' sates than all the rest o' the church putt together.

He went to no end o' trouble and bother about his choir; practise two nights a wik, tryin' to larn us how to zing the words

2

and chune at the zame time. He choosed out all the chaps with high squaiky voices to be the tinners, and they with gurt coose voices was spaused to zing baaze. The boyes and maidens was the tribbles, and all the ole women he putt back out o' zight and called them the allto. He obtained proper bukes vor the choir, with the chunes all printed with li'l black spots rinnin' up and down. They what knowed a bit o' music zinged by their notes, and the rest zinged by their yers. Zome aw'm pretended they was zingin' by music when they did'n know no more about it than a cat knows about his gran'mother. Fust time I yeard 'em tellin' about their D sharps and their B flats I said, 'That id'n right sort o' language to be usin' in Church Vestry.'

Timothy Daw, the shoemaker, reckoned he knowed all there was to know about zingin' by music. ''Tis cheel's play,' he said. 'All you've got to do is to go up when the notes goes up, and go down when they goes down.'

'If you was to watch Timothy while he was zingin' you cude zee he was carr'in' out his awn instructions, 'cus he used to move his haid up and down accordin' to the heighth o' the notes. If he got sevver'l notes gwain up, one arter t'other, you'd zee his ole neck stretchin' out like injy-rubber, and gettin' longer and longer as the notes rised higher and higher, till you cude'n zee nort of his face but the under part of his cheen. If he got another one or two arter that he'd have to rise up on tippy-toes, and people in the congregation wude be zayin' that if Timothy's chune did'n come down purty quick he'd get his neck bones out o' joint.

Anyway, our choir reckoned to zing in vower parts. Zometimes 'twas more than vower, but that was only when zomebody got gwain a bit zideways, like. When us was properly in the mood vor it, and got hold to zummat that us cude let go to, I dunnaw what you cude liken it to egsac'ly. There was nothin' to titch it anywhere around thase parts, and as for Stoke Arrish, they wadn't in it. They done the best they cude, but twas like a cat meowin' bezide a cow belvin' to compare they with we.

However, us had one very speshull occasion when the Bishup come out to Pitt to dessicrate the new bells; and the paasen decided the choir shude zing a antum Gived it out in the polepit, he did, wiks bevorehand, and announced that he shude want extry choir-practise, to larn the way to do it proper.

Zome o' the oldest parrishioners shaked their haids about it, and old Napper Sage told 'em straight out, twude bring trouble on the parrish, zeein' what happened the time bevore. But the choir had got their blid up by thees time, and there was no turnin' 'em from it.

'What's a antum, if you knows music?' says ole Timothy Daw. 'I'll guarantee I'd zing a antum all by mezelf, with one hand behind me back, if I'd got the notes.' And when they axed Georgie Lomas, the orgin-player, if he thought the choir was capable to zing a antum, he said:

'Ant-um! Ees. Uncle-um too, if necessary.'

However, when us come to zot about 'en, 'twad'n quite so aisy as zome aw'm tried to make out. Fer one thing us found there was a solo to 'en. Us did'n know what a solo was till the paasen explained 'twas for one body to zing a verse by hiszell. Soon as Susan Bidgude yeard that, her stood up and said her'd zing 'en. But paasen said it had to be a man's voice, for which us was very thankful, 'cus Susan have got a rare vine voice fer fetchin' in the cows when they'm a long distance away, but beyond that there id'n a lot to be said in favour aw't. When they said it mus' be a man, Timothy Daw rised up and said, 'You laive it to me. I'll let 'em know about solo.'

However, that wude'n do neether, 'cus it had to be baaze, zeem-zo, and o' coorse, Timothy's tinner. So there 'twas again.

'Must be eether Stephen Yeo, or Dicky Wesscott,' says Georgie Lomas.

Stephen Yeo got up.

'What do 'ee mean, Dicky Wesscott? Darn 'ee, I'd zing Dicky Wesscott's haid off.'

You zee, Stephen's the blacksmith, and half as big again as Dicky; so poor Dicky cude'n say nothin'. Therefore, 'twas decided that Stephen Yeo shude zing the solo.

The trouble the paasen and Georgie had to larn 'en the chune was nuff to break their heart. Stephen wude try 'en over and over till he considered he'd got 'en off, and then us wude zing the choriss part till it come to Stephen's turn. By that time he'd clane fergot it, and the chune he started wad'n nothin' like it. 'Twas a wearisome job, and if Stephen had only been a size or two smaller he'd have had to yer about it. However, his wive was in the choir, and her's purty quick at pickin' up a chune, so her said her'd larn it to him home. The noises that come from the blacksmith's houze fer the nex' night or two wude make 'ee think they was killin' pigs.

4

Our antum was the talk of all the neighbour'ude, and when the day come to zing 'en bevore the Bishup people walked fer miles to yer 'en. Most all the Stoke choir was present, and they went and sot theirzel's where Stephen cude'n help viewin' 'em, 'cus they thought that wude putt 'n off his stroke. I'm 'feared the volks did'n pay much attention to the fus' part o' the sarvice. They was all lookin' vor the antum, and the choir did'n know how to sit in their sates. And presen'ly us all stood up to let go at 'en.

The beginnin' part, which us zinged altogether, went very well, I believe. I was told it cude be heard over tother zide o' the railway. Napper Sage said he yeard it where he was lied a-bed, and that's half a mile off, near nuff. And Stephen's solo wude 'a-bin all right, I dersay, but for a bit of a accident, which nobody cude'n fore-zee.

Stephen's gurt trouble was to know jis' when to begin, and zo him and Georgie Lomas fixed it up between 'em, that when 'twas time fer Stephen to start, Georgie shude turn around in his sate and nod his haid. Drec'ly he done that Stephen was to start zingin' and go on till he'd vinished. Then us wude all join in the choriss again, and zing what was left.

That was all well and gude, but unforchnitly, jus' at the very wrong time, when the fus' choriss was gwain along nice, Georgie was took with a sneeze comin' on. Without meanin' any harm, he turned his haid around a bit, so's not to sneeze all over the orgin kays. Stephen was watchin' the orgin-player like a cat watchin' a mouze, swattin' straimes, 'fraid he wude'n come in zac'ly right. The minute Georgie's haid beginned to turn, Stephen tooked in a long breath, all in readiness, and presen'ly down went the orgin player's haid to sneeze, but the baaze zinger thought 'twas his nod, and he let out his fus' note like the roar of a bull.

'Twas too zoon, by a long lot, and the rest o' the choir was so tooked aback that half aw'm stapped zingin' and tother half went all wrong, and Georgie stapped the orgin. But Stephen did'n know. He was lettin' into it to such extaint he cude'n tell whether anythin' else was gwain on or no. And if he'd carr'd on and gone droo wai't, twude 'a-bin all right, cus nobody wad'n aware what was the matter seps the choir, and only half o' they. But Martha Yeo cud'n leave it alone. Her lained across with her buke and give her ole man a pug in the back. Stephen stap short and turned around to zee what was wrong, and I thought fer a minute the ole antum was gwain to finish with the zame. However, passen had the presence o' mind to tell Stephen to carry on, but the poor feller had forgot where he leaved off to, and he started on the wrong note, and lost his words, and had to zing "la la" to it. Instaid o' gwain down very low, as he was suppaused to, he'd got all up high, and the more he tried to rectify it the higher he went. I'll make a bet there was never a solo zinged like that one bevore. All the blid rished up into Stephen's haid, and the veins in his neck was like gas-pipes. So then Georgie gived the signal fer the rest o' the choir to come in with the choriss. Us zinged zomethin', but whether 'twas the antum or no I wud'n like to zay. And when the orgin stapped us stapped, and then us sot down.

'Twas a pity it happened like it, 'cus us wanted to let the Stoke volks zee how deep down Stephen cude go, and he did'n go down at all; he went up.

And what do Stoke do then but go and have a antum o' their awn, with a solo zinged by David Sprag. 'Twas as unfair as ever cude be, 'cus David had a cold on his chest and zo he was able to zing baaze a lot better than he can ordnery. Therefore they reckoned that Stoke Arrish bate Pitt Wollidge in the matter o' zingin', and comin' on top of all their other insults 'twas more'n flesh and blid cude stand. And that's railly what led up to the zingin' match.

2.   THE COMMITTEE

Zinging they two antums, to Pitt Woollidge and Stoke Arrish, zeemed to bring all the jellisness between the two villages to a head; like puttin' a poultice on it. After that 'twas nothin' but envy, hatred and mallish. Only, from that day forth, all the argimentation was about the zingin'. Us did'n bother no more about which parish cude win the tug-o'-war, or the skittles, or which cude produce the fastest runner or the highest jumper, or which drinked the most cider per haid o' the popilation, nor nothin' like that. 'Twas only which parish had the bes' notion o' zingin'. Stoke said they cude whack Pitt into a cocked 'at at it, and Pitt reckoned they cude zing Stoke out o' zight. Any stranger visitin' eether village wude yer nothin' else.

The most place for that kind o' talk was into the Spotted Tadpole. You'd get it there every aiv'min o' the wik, 'ammer and tongs.

You zee, the Spotted Tadpole is right on the boundary between the two parrishes, so the congregation that meets in there is half an' half; half Stoke and half Pitt. Consequently they cude argify all night, 'cus when one got out o' breath there was a dizzen more ready to take on.

One aiv'min, when there was a full party into the Spotted Tadpole, a couple o' strange gen'lmen looked een. Zummat had gone wrong with their moter, zeem-zo, arter coming up over the long hill. I understood one' o' the gen'lmen to zay the car had over-eat hiszelf. I dunnaw how that cude be, zac'ly, 'cus I wad'n aware that moters tooked solid food. I cude understand it if he'd over-drinked hiszelf. However, he'd recover all right if he rested a li'l while, by all accounts, so they come in and sot down a bit.

Come from Plymouth, they did, but they was rale gen'lmen, all the same for that. Lookid around the company, they did, to zee whose jugs was empty, and poor old Luke Shapter purt' near bust a blid-vessel lettin' back a quart all in one breath, 'fraid he'd be left out.

For a wonder us did'n hap'm to be arg'ing at the moment they come een, and I don't suppause us wude have started, not bevore strangers, only one aw'm hap'm to ketch zight o' the bill about our conzert comin' off to Pitt, and he remarked upon it.

'I zee you've got a conzert comin' off he said. 'Us must come out and yer that. Have 'ee got any gude zingers?'

Very wist thing he cude have said, with all they Stoke chaps presint, 'cus Stoke people ab'm got no more manners than a pig. 'Twas puttin' match to gun-powder. Bevore us had time to tell 'em what vine zingers there was to Pitt the Stoke chaps started cheemin' in with a pack o' lies.

'Shude'n take trouble to come out and yer that, if I was you, mister,' says one aw'm. 'Better by half bide home and harken to the trains up to North Road station, or the Devonport tram gwain round a corner. 'Twude save 'ee expainse, and be a lot more pleasant than Pitt zinging.'

Well, o' coorse, the fat was in the vire drec'ly. No Pitt body cude stand a-onezide and yer things like that said, strangers or no strangers. You never yeard sitch a shindy as there was vor the nex' vive minutes. Everybody was holleyin', one across tother, and nobody harkening; and the names they was callin' one-tother made me ashamed for what the two gen'lmen wude think

7

of us. However, they did'n zim to mind very much. Matter o' fac', they looked to be enjoyin' it, and when the racket beginned to die back a bit one aw'm made up a bit of a spaich.

''Tis no business o' mine', he says, 'and I don't want to interfere with your li'l frien'ly talks, but it zeems to me this is a very important matter which ought to be settled once and for all. What you want is a contest.'

'What zort o' thing's that, maister?' says ole Zammy Bryant.

'Well, a competition. Both zides putt out their best zingers, and zee which is champion.'

'You mean a zingin' match.'

'That's right; a zingin' match.'

My dear days, there was a hullaballoo, drec'ly. The words was no zooner mentioned than they was in everybody's mouthe. A zingin' match! The very thing.

David Sprag wanted to have it there and then, right away, and the rest o' the Stoke chaps backed him up. That was becus Stephen Yeo and one or two more o' the best Pitt zingers did'n hap'm to be present. That's jis' the zort o' durty trick they'm capable of. But the gen'lman putt the stopper on that.

''Tis too important to settle on the spurt o' the moment like that,' he says. 'You must have it carr'd out proper, in public, so's everybody can know there id'n no jiggery-pokery about it. 'Twill all have to be prepared bevore'and, and everybody mus' be brought acquainted with the date when 'tis comin' off, and they'll have to pay zixpence to go een. 'Twill be a big thing, mind, and the money can be give to the 'ospital.'

One or two aw'm beginned to dray in their horns when they yeard that. Tom Chick said 'twas makin' a mountain out of a want-heap, and Albert Partridge axed who did they think was gwain to pay money to yer that ole noise? Both o' they belongs to Pitt, so David Sprag says drec'ly:

'Pitt's afeard, lookee. They can't face it, 'cus they knows very well they'd be bate.'

Then there was another vine ole rabble, and o' coorse, arter that nobody did'n dare say a word agin it, else it wude be said they was frightened. Zo the two gen'lmen carr'd on with the transaction, and I cude zee they was jist about injoyin' theirzel's, the both aw'm. The one what done most o' the talkin' was called Mr. Jackson. I didn't ketch tother feller's name.

'Well, now,' said Mr. Jackson, 'the fust thing is to have a committee, and as you zeems to be purty well equal from the two parishes, I propose that those presint in the rume now forms the committee.'

'Cude'n do better, I daun' reckon,' says Tom Chick, who wanted to get back in the click again, when he zee'd which way things was gwain. Zo that was agreed upon.

'Now you'll need a cheerman,' says Mr. Jackson, 'and you want to try to choose out zomebody what won't favour one zide more'n tother.'

'You carry on as you be, zur,' says Albert Partridge. 'You'm doin' very well, and I propose you for cheerman.'

Everybody was in favour o' that, zo 'twas carr'd anominously.

'Well, now,' he says, 'what's the fus' business?'

'To zee all the jugs be full,' says Timothy Daw. That caused a bit of a laaf and helped to shift off zome o' the bad-friendship between the two parties. When that job was zee'd to, the cheerman said:

'Now, what's the nex' business?'

'To zee they'm all empty agean,' says Sammy Bryant. That shifted all the bad-friendship there was left.

'Stiddy on a bit,' says cheerman, 'there's a lot to be done bevore us comes to that. I've got a sheet o' paper yer and us'll write down all the rules. Fust. "Zingin'" Match, open only to the parishes of Stoke Arrish and Pitt Wollidge, to be held on sitch-an'-sitch a date at sitch-an'-sitch a place." Us can dezide on the when's and the where's arter us have finished with the whys and the wherefores. Now the nex' thing. How many from each village shall take part?'

'I shude zay, all the parish,' says Tom Chick. "Twude'n be fair, else.'

'Giddout. That waun' do,' says David Sprag. 'Who's gwain to harken, if everybody be zingin'?'

'Who wants to harken?' says Tom. 'The prize is for zingin', not harkenin'.'

'I don't think it cude be all the parish,' says Mr. Jackson, 'although I shude very much like to zee it, mezelf. But I doubt if you'd get everybody to take part, and if you was to you wude'n have no gate money.'

Timothy Daw spoked up. 'I reckon it ought to be one picked out to represent each parish. I don't mind zingin' fer Pitt.'

'Rummage!' says Albert Partridge. 'If anybody zings for Pitt, it shude be Stephen Yeo.' That started argiment amongs' all the Pitt lot. Timothy zee'd there was more for Stephen than what there was for he,

9

so he gived up the idaya of only one, and advocated it shude be the choir from each parish.

'I think that's a very gude suggestion,' says cheerman. 'The choir from each parish to compete. They ought to form theirzels into a choral society for the occasion, and add on fresh zingers so's to take in the chapel bodies as well, and larn the speshul chunes. But us wants to vind the bes' zinger out of the two parishes as well, zo you wants two classes; one vor the bes' choir and one vor the bes' zinger. Each parish cude enter as many zingers as they mind to, only they'd have to zing one to a time, and the best o' the lot wude be champion.'

Everybody thought that was a very suitable idaya, and 'twas decided accordin'.

'The nex' thing is,' says cheerman, 'who shall us have for jidge?'

That got 'em all quiet fer a bit, and 'twas cruel to zee how hard they was thinkin'. At last Timothy Daw said:

Do us need to have a jidge?'

'Of coorse us must have a jidge,' says Mr. Jackson. 'How can us gwain to tell which is the better zingers else?'

'Any fule can tell 'ee that Pitt is better zingers than Stoke,' says Timothy. 'You don't want no jidge for that.'

My stars, that purt' near finished up the meetin', and it took the cheerman all his time to get 'em back to order again. And I wude'n zay he'd ever have done it, only Sam Bryant missed his beer all of a sudden, and thought zomebody else had drinked it. Sammy's voice very soon drowned all the rest. Then 'twas discovered the beer wad'n drinked, but the lan'lord noticed the jug was in danger o' bein' knacked over in the excitement, so he'd shifted it back to another table. So then the cheerman was able to get in a word.

'Of coorse us must have a jidge, else people wude zay 'twad'n jonnick. The thing is, who can us agree upon?'

'What about Mr. George Atwude?' says Wi'yum Smale. 'He've acted as jidge to all the shows around these parts vor years, and alwis give satsifaction so-fur as I know. I've never yeard nothin' to the contr'y.'

'A very gude man,' says Albert. 'You won't better 'en.' And sevver'l others said the zame.

'Is this Mr. Atwude a gude jidge o' music?' says Mr. Jackson.

'I never yeard that he done much in that line,' says Wi'yum, 'but he's as gude a jidge o' pigs as you'll vind in the county; and I reckon if a man have got sainse nuff to jidge pigs he ought to be able to jidge zingin'.'

That was the general opinion o' the meetin', but the cheerman did'n vall in wai 't.

'Fer one thing,' he says, 'I expec' you'd vind Mr. Atwude wude rayfuse to take it on. To jidge proper a man must know all the ins and outs o' what he'm jidgin'. Now, I'm acquainted with a gen'lman into Plymouth what is accustomed to that zort o' thing, and is a gurt musicker hiszelf. If you was agreeable, I think I cude persuade he to come and do the jidgin'.'

That was a cabbical idaya, and 'twas carr'd accordin'.

'What points will 'em be jidged upon?' axed Tom Chick.

'Well,' says Mr. Jackson, 'on gude zingin', of coorse.'

'That depends on what you calls gude zingin',' says Tom. 'Us had a wumman come out to Pitt skule-rume to zing once. Cracked up to be zummin wonderful, her was, such a zinger as never had bin bevore. Squire paid I dunnaw how much money to have her out yer to zing, but I daun' reckon her was worth a flip. I wude'n go the length o' me nose to harken to such ole yaalin' and zammy-quavering. I likes zummat with a bit of a rattle to it.'

'Should be the one what can be yeard the furthest away, I reckon,' says Albert.

'No,' says Wi'yum. 'The lot what can last out the longest wude be most fairest.'

Then the cheerman said, 'I think us ought to laive all that to the jidge.' And when us come to think it over, that zeemed as gude a way as any.

By this time the two gen'lmen's moter had recovered from his over'eatin', so they sot out fer Plymouth. And when they wished us 'Gudenight,' they said they was lookin' vorward to the zingin' match.

I'll bet they was, too.

3.   HAIL, SMILING MORN

'I've witnessed a vew kick-ups of one zort and another in my time, what with Pitt Revel, and Vith o' November and Club Walk, and the Wile Baiste Show and such like; but for the quantity of excitement in the space of time, I reckon the Zingin' Match

11

whacked the lot of 'em. There's never been nothin' to aiqual it anywhere around this part o' the co'ntry.

Mind you, takin' everything into consideration, I dunnaw that 'tis the zort o' thing I shude recommend other parishes to take up. Not in the zame way as us done it. I won't zay but what a zingin' match might be all well and gude if 'twas carr'd out vitty, and everything done in proper order. But to get that you must have the right volks at the haid of affairs; not go lettin' every Dick, Tom and 'Arry have his say in the matter.

That's what the trouble was with our zingin' match; 'twas in the wrong hands. O' coorse, they two gen'lmen from Plymouth was only out for a bit o' fun. They zee'd the chance to have zome sport, and that's all they was after. They didn't care which parish was best singer, no more than my boot. 'Twas the chaipest intertainment ever they had, and I'll make a bet thay've had many a gude laaf auver it since.

Where us made the fus' mistake to was to go formin' the committee and makin' arrangements into the Spotted Tadpole, without consultin' any other body. What us ought to a-done, and us cude zee it when 'twas too laate, as soon as the thing was fus' started us ought to have went straight to the fountain-haid in each parish and got the paasens and a vew o' the bettermost volk to take it up bevore us went so fur with it.

As 'twas, us went to they zort o' people arterwards and told 'em us had got a committee and this, that and tother, and decided all manner o' things, and then axed they to join een. So 'twas only natteral they shude turn around and zay, 'You've done so well up to now, you'd better-way go on and finish it, and us'll come and look on.'

And that's what they *did* zay, wan and all. Very near knacked the whole thing in the haid, that did, and if the committee had been all of one parish, 'tis my belief 'twude have been the finisher. But being half of Pitt Wollidge and half of Stoke Arrish, neether zide did'n like to advocate jackin' it up, 'cus tothers wude zay drec'ly they was 'feared they was gwain to be bate. Zo us carr'd on as best as us cude.

Mr. Jackson and tother Plymouth gen'lman come out a time or two to our committee meetin's to instruct us the right way to go to work. And once they took out this-yer Mr. Crochet, the musickin' gen'lman what was gwain to be the jidge. Very nice gen'lman he was too, and very clever at music I shude think, 'cus his hair come all down over his coller behind. He had a speshul meetin' with Georgie Lomas and Charlie Diment. They'm the two laiders, see, 'cus Georgie plays the orgin to Pitt and Charlie to Stoke. They understan's all about music and they can tell one chune from another by only lookin' to they li'l black spots with the long tails.

Mr. Crotchet termed George and Charlie the 'conducters,' and wad'n they some plaised, begad.

Mr. Crotchet let the conducters have the chunes which he'd choosed out fer the zingin' match. That was what he called the test pieces. Everybody had to zing the test piece, and also one zong of his own choosin'. What I mean to zay, they had to zing Mr. Crotchet's zong fust and then they cude zing what zong they liked arter that. They was new names to me, they test pieces was. The baazes had to zing one called 'Down amongst the daid men,' and the tinners, 'Where my Carrier's Van has rested.' The chune fer the choirs to zing altogether was called, 'Hail, smilin' morn.'

I noticed both Charlie Diment and Georgie Lomas lookin' down over their noses when they zee'd this-yer music. I reckon 'twas a trifle beyond what they'd bin accustomed to. However, neether-one of 'em did'n like to be the fust to zay so, and when Mr. Crotchet axed 'em if that wude be all right they both said, 'Ees.' They'd larn the chunes to the ones what had got to zing 'em, zo they said. And they tried to zay it as if they cude do it on their 'aids.

But I'm jiggered if they hadn't got their work cut out for the nex' vew wiks, till come time for the match. So fur as Georgie was consarned I know fer a fact that it purt' near putt 'n in lunatic asylum, and I understand Charlie wad'n no better. Both aw'm went right off their food, and very near off their beer.

In the fus' plaace, it tooked Georgie I dunnaw how long to larn the chunes hiszelf, never mind about larnin' 'em to any other body. He was hummin' 'em over mornin', noon and night. Wan aiv'min George's wive come rishin' up to our houze and said to my missis:

'Let me come and zit down along o' you fer a nower, there's a dear zaul, for if I bides in the houze along of my ole man another minute I shall go daaft, I know I shall. What with he playin' they chunes with one vinger and tryin' to zing 'em at the zame time, I'm gettin' the jumps.'

13

Zo you can jist imagine what 'twas vor poor ole Timothy Daw and Stephen Yeo when they come to larn their zongs. Stephen was one o' the heftiest men in the village when he started, but I'm jiggered if it did'n nearly pull he down to a skeleton, till the volks beginned to zay if he zinged it at all 'twude be with a harp in his hand. As fer Timothy, he wad'n very much more than a skeleton to start wai', so they reckoned he'd disappear altogether.

When the ole choral party started on with their 'Hail, smilin' morn,' 'twas a buster. James Way said 'twas nuff to make it snow, never mind about hail. They used to do their practisin' in the skule-rume, and if anybody outzide had'n knowed better they'd have said 'twas zomebody bein' muddered, or else a litter o' pigs bein' ringed.

Scritchin'! Holleyin'! Groanin'! Startin' in the wrong place. Gwain back to the beginnin' and startin over again. Gettin' in a mix-muddle. Gettin out o' that into a worse one. Blamin' it on to the chap in front or the wumman behind. Georgie whackin' the deskis with his stick and baalin' out:

'Tribbles, hold yer noise till the tinners have zinged a bar. Baazes start on the third bate. That wad'n the third, can't 'ee count? Now then, come on tribbles. Shut up, tinners, tid'n your turn now. Let into it, baazes. Never mind the words; la-la it; allto's, zing yer own notes and laive the tribbles' alone. Now let rip, altogether, "Darkness flies away!" Can't 'ee make more noise than that? Now, come on tinners, "Flies away!" Now, baazes, "Flies away!" No! Not fly away altogether; one after the tother.'

I tell 'ee, 'twas better 'n any pantomime. Crowds use to stand outzide in the road to harken, 'cus all manner o' funny things wude hap'm zometimes. Once I remember a most hawful noise, with Mrs. Dobb's voice squawkin' up above all the rest, and all out o' chune, somethin' dreadful. George stapped 'em as soon as he cude make hiszelf yeard, and he says:

'What hever be you zingin' of, Mrs. Dobbs?'

'I'm zingin' what's wrote down yer with the intention for me to zing, Mr. Lomas,' her says, very haughty. Mrs. Dobbs thinks a tremenjis lot of her zingin' I might tell 'ee, and she reckons she's one o' the very few what zings by the music.

'But there id'n no high notes like that, all up where you be to.'

'Yes, there is, Mr. Lomas, *and* sevver'l more to come.'

Georgie went to look at her paaper.

14

'Caw, bless my zaul, Mrs. Dobbs, you'm on the wrong page. All the rest have turned over long ago.'

And Mrs. Dobbs says, as if her was a duchess talkin' to the man that come fer the rabbit-skins:

'The rest must do as they plaise, Mr. Lomas. I shall turn over when I comes to the bottom o' the page, and *not bevore!*'

And sure nuff, Liza Dobbs carr'd on with her zingin', or what her subs'ichutes for zingin' till her considered her'd vinished out that page, and then her turned over to the next.

So you can quite understand Georgie had got a job on. One of his wist troubles was to get 'em all to stap together when they come to the end. So he gived out this notice:

'When I holds up my stick like that, and waggles it about, so, that means there's only one more rap to go. When I gives it a whack on the desk, that means 'Stap.' Everybody must stap to-once, 'cus they ought to be to the finish. Anybody what ab'm reached the finish must let the rest go. If anybody have finished before I gives the signal they'd better-way go back and zing the last line over agean.'

When I tells 'ee that Charlie Diment was havin' the zame barney over to Stoke, you must imagine what the match was like.

The Gurt Zingin' Match between Pitt Wollidge and Stoke Arrish was held in the vield back o' the Spotted Tadpole, of a Wainsdy aiv'min. Hunderds o' volks was there, 'cus the match was a table-talk for miles around. Zixpence a-piece they paid to go een, excep' they what climmed in over Farmer Blackmore's orchard hedge. When I tell 'ee that arter payin' all expenses us gived vive pound to the Cottage 'Ospital you must know us had a middlin' gude crowd. Us had a vine gurt platvorm fer the zingers to stand upon, and a aisy cheer fer the jidge, with a li'l table in front to rest his paapers on. Zome o' the onlookers was fer Pitt and zome was fer Stoke, and a gude many was fer whatever amusement they cude get out of it.

As to the zingin' part o' the business, I can't zay very much. George and Charles tossed up for which village shude go fust, and Georgie winned. That started a row drec'ly. George reckoned if he winned he had the right to make Stoke go fust, and Charlie said 'No, the winner must start.' So they putt it to the jidge, and he said Pitt was to start.

So the Pitt lot got top the platvorm to zing 'Hail, smilin' morn.' The remarks o' the Stoke chaps as each one stepped up was nuff to

15

confuse anybody, and the consequence was when George had waved his stick about and counted vower only one body started, and that was Mrs. Dobbs with imitation of a train whistle. Everybody bust out laafin'.

However, George counted vower more and started zingin' hiszelf, so the rest graj'ly joined een. When they got warmed up they let into it fine, only, of coorse, a gude many was late startin' so they never properly ketched up. So they was doin' their 'Flies away' long arter the rest had flied away and was zingin' someplace else. Spaikin' for my own part, I dunnaw what the chune ought to zound like, and therefore I ban't capable to zay whether 'twas right or wrong. All I know is, that arter the choir had finished and the jidge had got back his breath, he axed Georgie Lomas whether that was the test piece, or their own choosing.

Georgie said, 'That was "Hail, smilin' morn," zur.'

'Aw, thank you,' says the jidge. 'That's all I wanted to know.'

However, all the Pitt volk gived the choir a gude clap when they'd vinished, and then the Stoke lot got up and zinged.

They got away to the start better than what us did, I will zay that vor 'em, and I was 'fraid o' me life they was gwain right droo wai'out mistaake. But they hadn't got very fur bevore they was forced to stap, by reason of quarr'ling amongs' theirzel's. David Sprag started it by axin' Peter Choke what for gudeness saake he thought he was doin'.

'I'm zingin',' says Peter, 'but I dunnaw what you be up to.'

'Zingin', do 'ee call it?' says David. 'My dog wude make a better noise than that.'

'Tell 'ee the truth I thought it *was* your dog when you started,' says Peter. Then there was a middlin' vine rumpus. And mind you, this was right in the middle o' the chune, zo they all had to stap till David and Peter had zettled the matter. The only way they cude do that was to putt 'em further apart, 'cus David said he cude'n zing with that buzzin' row gwain on all the time in his yer-ole. Arter that they made a proper mess o' the job, 'cus one half o' the zingers considered they had to go back to the beginnin' and start afresh, and tother hald thought they had to go on where they leaved off to. They did'n discover what was the matter till the fus' lot had come to the end o' the chune and found that the rest had only jus' reached the middle. Then none of 'em knowed what to do. Some o' the second lot stapped, and some went on. Then some more stapped, and it graj'ly got thinner and thinner till only David Sprag was left by all hiszelf. He determined to finish it out, but o' coorse, when he 'Flied away,' he had to wait while the tinners 'Flied away.' But they'd all flied away and gone, so the poor feller was done, and the chune finished up like the dyin' pig.

All the Pitt lot was roarin' laafin' and makin' all manner o' noises like cats yaalin' and dogs howlin' and hens and ducks. And with two or dree free fights gwain on into the bargin, I'm jiggered if it wad'n a middlin' vine racket fer a bit.

Then Stephen Yeo was suppaused to come on and zing. 'Down amongst the daid men.' 'Twas announced that he wude do zo, but when Stephen got up top the platvorm, his heart failed 'n, and he started to zing 'The Vacant Cheer,' and as Georgie Lomas was playin' the other chune on the pianner, 'twas a middlin' vine scummer. The Stoke chaps started to zing 'Cat's got the maisles.' Completely drowned poor Stephen, and all of a sudden he jumped down off the platvorm, picked out the ringlaider and give 'n a gude leatherin'.

After that 'twas a job to tell what was gwain on egzac'ly. There was so much argifyin' and yappin' amongs' the crowd 'twas impossible to yer the zingin'. However, the program was all finished to-last, and then everybody was aiger to yer what the jidge had to zay. Us had'n gived he a thought fer ever so long, 'cus us had bin so intent on givin' our own opinions us had'n troubled about no other body's.

When us wanted the jidge us cude'n vind 'n no-place. Nor Mr. Jackson. Nor tother feller. When us inquired of Bill Burge, who was in charge o' the gaate, Bill said:

"Tis no gude you lookin' vor they. All dree aw'm went off in their moter full speed half-a-nower agone. By the way they was trav'lin', I shude zay they'm to P'ymouth by now.'

THE LIKENESS TAKER

'Tis amazin' how anybody can cause trouble and strife zometimes, when they did'n mean nothin' but kindness. Us had a case like that once when my darter Jane was livin' home along o' me and mother, bevore her got married.

Jane had one o' they likeness-taking contraptions sent to her for birthdy present by her Uncle Ben up to Lunnon. Ben done it with the very best intentions, and wraut a nice letter wishin' the maid many 'appy returns o' the day. But I'm blest if he did'n come very near to bustin' up a 'appy home instead.

'Twas tremenjis excitement when Jane undone the paacel and took out this-yer likeness-taker, or caramel as they calls it. Ansum lookin' thing, 'twas, and must 'a-cost a middlin' scute o' money. One o' they pull-in-an'-out ones he was, like Jim Cann's accorjeon, with a lot o' li'l doors and winders, and silvery nobs and all manner o' gadjits. When he was all shut up he'd go in yer pocket, aisy, but when he was opened proper he stretched out to ever such a long length, and then us cude take people's images with 'n. At laiste, so 'twas said. But the fust day or two I thought us wude be more likely to take leave of our sainses.

As I zay, he lookid very smart when the maid took 'en out o' the paacel, and what a weight, compared with the size. Us was all surprised at the heft aw'n, and us agreed he mus' be a gude one to weigh so heavy. Bein' all closed up flat, he didn' look nothin' like a likeness machine, and me and mother cude'n make haid ner tail aw'n. Mother considered 'twas zome new-fangled sort o' ladies' bag, and said there would be a brish and comb and all such like inzide, and a lookin'-glass; but I reckoned 'twas a money-box. However, the maid knowed what was comin' to her, zeem-zo, and her told us 'twas a caramel.

18

'What can 'ee do with 'n, now you've got 'n?' says mother.

'Take people's likeness with 'n,' says the maid.

'Rummage,' says mother. 'How can 'ee take people's likeness with a thing like that? He ab'm got no legs.'

'This sort don't have legs,' says Jane. ''Tis a hand caramel.'

'Where's his hands to, then?' mother axed her. 'I don't zee neether hands ner legs. I've had my likeness took times enough, and I knows very well it requires a thing big enough fer the chap to get his haid and shoulders into. And he've got a round winder in front for 'ee to look pleasant into.'

'So have this one got a round winder.'

'What, that li'l hole? That wude'n take the tip of anybody's nose.'

'You wait a bit and zee,' says Jane.

'I shall have to wait a long time bevore I zees anybody's image come out of a trumpery li'l thing like that.'

'You shude'n zay such things bevore you knows,' I says. 'You can't zay what can be done.'

'No,' her says, 'but I can zay what can't be done, and I'm purty sure you can't make a likeness with thik fiddlin' li'l contraption.'

'He'm a lot bigger than this when he'm open,' says the maid.

'Well, ope' min, and let's zee.'

'Twas aisy nuff to zay ope' min, but 'twas a differ'nt matter when us come to try. There was lots o' li'l nobs and hannles about, of one zort and another, and us tried pushin' this one, and squaisin' that one, but nort did'n hap'm worth mentionin'. All of a sudden mother titched zummat by accident, and bothered if the front part did'n open. Her did'n know how her done it, no more than the dead, but her pretended her did.

'You wants to use yer gumtion a bit,' her says. 'I knows more about it than the two of 'ee putt together.'

However, he wad'n open proper, only loppin' out all anyhow.

'Come on, then, ' I said to mother. 'Finish it while you'm about it.'

'Finish it yerzell,' her says. 'I've showed 'ee how to start; now 'tis for you to do the rest.'

Jane fiddled about a bit, and presen'ly her discovered the way to pull out the bellisses. That was a vine job, sure nuff.

'Us'll be able to play a chune purty quick,' I says. 'He's gettin' more like Jim Cann's accorjeon every day.'

19

'I can get on now, all right,' says Jane, "cus I've zee'd Mary Jinkins using hers. All you do's is to look in this-yer li'l winder and you can zee whatever you'm gwain to take. Then you've only got to squaise the injy-rubber ball and the pischer is took.'

'Sounds orright,' I says. 'Us'll go outdoors and take zummat.'

'Uncle Ben says on the letter 'tis in readiness to take zix picshers,' says Jane.

'Us can aisy vind zix differ'nt things to take,' I said. So us carr'd the ole caramel out in coort. In one minute the maid was shoutin' out, proper delighted.

'You can zee 'en butiful, dad. Jus' you look in thik li'l winder and you'll zee a lovely picsher.' So I tooked the caramel and keened into the li'l winder. I cud'n make out nothin' at fust, but all-to-once I ketched it proper. The caramel was lookin' towards the houze, and there was the picsher in the li'l winder as plain as a pike-staff. A teeny-weeny picsher, but you cude zee the doors and the winders and chumley, and the flowers and everything perfec'.

'There 'tis, jus' like life,' I said. 'What must us do to keep 'n there?'

'You hold 'n straight, and I'll squaise the li'l ball,' says Jane. So us done that, and I yeard 'n go click. I rished in-houze, like a cheel with a new toy.

"Tis right, mother,' I said. 'Jus' you come and look in this purty li'l picsher of the houze.'

But I'm beggered! When her come to look, he was gone.

'Yer, maid! Us have done zummat wrong. You did'n squaise 'n hard nuff.'

'Don't be silly,' her saith. 'That id'n where the photo comes to; you only looks in there to make sure he'm pointin' straight. The picsher comes in behind, zomewhere. When us have tooked all zix us mus' carr' the caramel into Peter Finnemore, into Barleycombe, 'cus they have to be done zummat to bevore they can be tooked out.'

Mother said, "Twude be a lot more sainse if you was to carry in the one you've done and zee if that's all right, bevore you attemp's the remainder.'

That zeemed a very gude idaya, so me and the maid drived into Barleycombe, to Peter Finnemore's chimis's shop, and explained what us wanted. But Peter reckoned he cude'n do nothin' till us had took all zix. From what I cude understand, they'm all attached together in a fillum, and 'tis a case of all or nort.

'Did you zay you'd tooked a picsher?' says Peter.

'Us have took one,' I told 'n.

'No, you ab'm,' he says.

'Yes us have, I tell 'e.' I thought 'twas like his chick to contridic' like that, when he wad'n there to zee.

'You can't have, 'cus the fillum id'n turned around, not 'eet.'

Made me look a bit of a fule, that did, and I wished I hadn't bin hardly so fast. Tid'n wise to have too much to zay when you'm dealin' with zummat you don't understand.

'You mus' screw around this-yer li'l hannle,' says Peter, 'till you zees the figger "One" in the li'l hole. There 'tis, lookee. And when you've took that one, you mus' screw 'n around agean till you zees vigger "Two".'

Zo us went back home to try agean, and when us explained to mother what us had larned, her said, 'I thought it mus' be zummat like that. Any fule cude zee thik hannle pokin' out, and if you'd axed me I shude have told 'ee to twist 'n around. You'd never have opened 'n at all if it hadn't bin fer me.'

'No,' I said, 'and you cude'n do it agean to zave yer life.'

'That's all the thanks I gets fer showin' 'ee,' says mother. 'Nex' time, I shall let 'ee vind out for yerzells.'

'Ees, I know you will,' I said.

'Be quiet, you two,' says the maid. 'What us knows all dree putt together don't amount to very much. But us can take the picshers and leave Mr. Finnemore to do the rest. What shall us take?'

'I shude take and wash up they durty dishes if I was you,' says mother. 'You wude know what you was about, anyway, and be doin' a bit o' gude.'

'Come on, mother, us'll take you fust,' says Jane.

'Not likely you wont. I shude look very nice, shude'n I, with me hair all rats' tails.'

'"Twaun' take 'ee a minute to putt that to-rights.'

'Think I ab'm got nort better to do this hower o' day than go wastin' me time on that ole trumpery?'

But all zame fer that, her flipped up over stairs and tettyvated herzell up a bit and putt on her bes' gown. Her pretended her intended doin' that in any case.

'I suppose I'd better-way come out jis' to plaise 'ee,' her saith, 'but I'll bet a guinea 'twill be a proper old fright, or most likely nothin' at all. 'Tis only a paacel of ole crams, all the lot aw't.'

Us had out a cheer from bes' kitchen and mother sot down and started puttin' her faace to-rights. 'Twude have made a cat laaf to zee all the antics her went droo. Fust her thought her'd have her hat on; then her did'n think her'd like that so well. Her'd be took without a hat. Then her'd like to be holdin' umberella; no, that wude look too stiff; her wude'n have no umberella. Did her ought to have her veet crossed or no?

'That don't make no odds,' I says, 'so long as you don't cross yer eyes.'

Nex' trouble was, the maid did'n know how fur away her ought to stand. I said I thought zomewhere down by the church gate, then her'd be well out o' zight.

'Do be quiet, vather,' her says. 'I shan't take none at all if you keeps on.'

'Do you think you'll take any if I leaves off?' I said.

Her aimed the ole caramel to mother and squaised the li'l ball and made 'n go 'click'.

'You ab'm been and done it, have 'ee?' says mother.

'Ees; of coorse I have.'

'Why did'n you tell me you was gwain to? I did'n have my face ready a bit. I wad'n aware the blessid thing was gwain pop like that. I thought you had to take off a thing in front. That's the way I've alwis been done bevore. I shall look a proper fright, I know I shall.

'That's all right,' I said. ''Tis a likeness us wants.'

Then the maid said her'd take one of mother stood up, and us had another ole caper while her choosed the best position for that. Her'd lain agin the cheer, like zo; no, her wude'n, her'd stand by the wall; no, her did'n like that; how did her look with one hand on the gaate?

'You wude'n believe me if I was to tell 'ee,' I said.

I shude like to be doin' zummat a bit out o' the ordnery,' says mother.

'Why daun' 'ee be took standin' on yer haid?' I said.

However, they got that one right to-last, and arter that Jane mus' take one of me and mother together, and one of me by mezell. And then I said, 'Have you been turnin' around thik li'l hannle all this time, which Peter Finnemore told about?'

'Aw, my blessid,' says the maid. 'I fergot all about that.'

'Then you've got all they vower picshers on top o' one-tother,' I said. ''Twill be a bit of a crowd.

And mother said, 'I thought you'd go and do that. I cude have told 'ee zo but you wude'n listen to me if I did. I'm certain sure you ban't gwain the right way to work, 'cus you ab'm used half they li'l nobs and things. They wude'n be there if they wad'n meant vor zummin. What's that one vor?'

Her titched a li'l thing pokin' out of the side, and 'click' he goes.

'Now you've bin and done it, mother,' says Jane.

'Time zomebody done zomething,' her says. 'I'll make a bet I've putt it to-rights now. He wude'n go "click" like that, unless he was intended to.'

'Well, zit down again, and I'll take 'ee proper.'

So mother sot down again, and arranged her faitures to her liking. Then I was told to zit down.

'Let me do this one,' says mother. 'If I can't make a better job aw't than you did, I'll eat the ole likeness-taker and the paper 'twas wrapped in.'

So I sot down, jus' to plaise 'em, and mother tooked the ole caramel. 'Now what is it I've got to do? Jis' squaise this-yer ball?' And with the zame her give 'n a squaise and 'click' goes the works.

'Mind what you'm about mother,' says Jane. 'You've been and took a photo.'

'Grammar! Took a photo! I ab'm aimed 'n yet.'

'That don't make no odds. You've took whatever you was aimin' at.'

'Don't tell up such rummage. 'Tis your vather I be gwain to take, id'n it, and I wad'n even lookin' that way.'

'But you muzzen squaise the ball till you'm aimin' at what you'm gwain to take.'

'I know that, don't I?'

'But you've click 'n already.'

'Don't be silly, cheel. That wad'n nothin'. I was only tryin' to zee if he was in workin' order. I did 'n squaise 'n hard.'

'Well, you've spoiled thik fillum, anyway,' says Jane.

'Hold thee tongue, spoiled the fillum! I ab'm touched the fillum. Now, zit up straight, vather, and try and not look as if

23

you'm gwain to be zick. Rin and get yer vather's walkin'-stick, Jane, and a differ'nt hat to that ole thing. Try and make 'n look dacent, if 'tis possible.'

So they gayked me up like a mommet. 'Now, mother,' says Jane, 'you aim 'en till you zees vather's image in the li'l winder.'

'I know, I know,' her says; and her was jis' gwain to squaise the ball.

'Yer,' I said. 'He id'n pointin' my way a bit.'

'You can't zee vather in the li'l winder, I'm sure,' says the maid.

'Bless yer zaul,' says mother, 'I can zee he plain nuff without lookin' in there. I can zee 'en with the naked eye.'

'But you can't take his likeness without you'm pointin' the caramel straight.'

'That's near nuff,' says mother. 'You'm too pa'ticler by half and that's why you waste so much time. Other volks don't take half so-long as you do.'

'Don't be redeclus, mother. You must have the thing pointin' straight.'

'So he is pointin' straight. How much more straighter than that do you want it?' With the zame her squaised the ball. 'There now, I'll make a bet that's the best o' the lot. There's nothin' in it if you uses your common-sainse.'

'I don't expec' there's very much in that one,' I said. 'I did'n veel nothin', anyway.'

'I wish I'd waited till there was zomebody to show us the way to do it proper,' says Jane.

'I don't zee what more you wants showin',' says mother. 'I never found the laistest difficulty.'

'Let me have a go at 'n,' I said. 'I'll bet a guinea I'll make a better fist aw't than eether one of 'ee. Zit down, maid, and I'll take you.'

So Jane her sot her down and I aimed 'n till I cude zee her in the li'l winder; and that very minute there came a click to the coort gaate. I turned right round, and who shude it be but paasen comin' een droo. How I come to do it I can't think, but I had the li'l ball in me vingers, and being a bit startled I s'pause to zee the paasen comin' unexpected, I squaised the ball without thinkin', and I yeard the blessid thing go 'click'. Nobody else did'n yer it, 'cus they was makin' so much noise.

'Caw,' I thought to mezell, 'I'd betterway turn that one around and zay nort about it.' So while mother and Jane was yappin' to

24

paasen I twisted the ole screw around and he come to number vive.

'What be you up to? Takin' photos, I zee,' says the paasen. 'You've got a butiful day vor it. Go on, don't let me interfere.'

So Jane sot down in cheer and I keened in the li'l winder and tried to look as if I knowed all about it. What a 'mazing thing it is, how us likes to make other volks imagine us be more wise than what us be. I spause us be all like it, more or less. Manys-a-times I've laafed at mother vor the zame thing, and now I was doin' it mezell. However, Jane sot up and tried to look purty, and when I'd got the ole caramel what I considered straight I squaised the ball and made 'n click.'

'That's a nice-lookin' caramel, says paasen, and tooked 'n in his hand.

'Jane had it gived her for a birthdy present,' says Ann. 'Us have took sevver'l likenesses, but of coorse us can't tell what they looks like, 'cus us don't know the way to get 'em out egzac'ly, though I dersay I cude vind out if I was to examine the thing proper.'

'But you ab'm got 'n sot right,' says paasen. 'You've got 'n sot vor twenty-vive voot and you'm only stood about ten voot away.'

'That's jus' what I thought', says mother. 'I told 'em they wad'n stood to the right plaace, but they thought they knowed best.'

'Aw, you'm stood about right,' he says, 'but you ought to have the bellises drayed out to a differ'nt place. There's li'l marks yer, look-zee, to show where you ought to fix 'en to, accordin' to the distance you'm stood away.'

'I knowed it must be somethin' like that,' says my Ann. 'Anybody can zee they li'l marks. But 'twas no use for me to zay aught. They wude 'n be guided by me.'

'Well, suppose you all get close together, and I'll take 'ee in a group,' says paasen. 'Have you turned around the fillum since you took the last one, Jan?'

'No, zur, I ab'm. I was jis' gwain to when you spoke.'

'Then you've jis' got one more left.'

'Two, there ought to be,' says Jane.

'This is number vive,' says paasen, 'and 'twill be zix when I turns 'en around.'

Jane cude'n fathom that. Her tried to reckon it up, and her cude'n make but vower aw't. I did'n think 'twas worth-a-while to let 'em know I'd turned one around unbeknown. However, paasen tooked the last one and then us carr'd the whole contraption to Peter Finnemore.

End o' the wik us had back the photos.

I shude zay there never was sitch picshers before nor since; and that you'd zay, if you was to zee 'em.

Where us had the vower all on the one fillum there was haids and veet all over the plaace, and 'twas impossible to make tap or tail aw't. I'd defy anybody to tell which was upzide-down ad which was downzide-up. The nex' one was where mother titched the li'l nob bevore the time, and her tooked a butiful likeness of the ole sow, which happened to be in the coort at the time. Then Jane tooked mother on the zame picsher, and I'm beggered if you wude'n sware mother was sot on the ole sow's back. Then there was suppaused to be one of me, but mother had squaised the baal bevorehand and took a photo of the roof o' the houze. Her did'n point the nex' one straight, so all there as o' me was two gurt feet, one each zide o' the chimley. My one o' Jane wude 'a-bin all right, only the bellises wad'n vitty, so her was all misky. The one the paasen took was all right so-fur as it went, but us was all dree lookin' as if us expected to vall dead the nex' minute.

But the mos' marvellous thing o' the lot was a butiful picsher o' the paasen comin' in droo the gaate. 'Twas perfec'. Paasen said hiszell he never zee'd nothin' better.

I done that. But nobody wude'n give me no praise vor it, 'cus they said I done it accidental. And that's the way o' this world, all over.

26

THE WORKING MODEL

I zee'd ole Silas Wonnacott laafin' to hiszell when zomebody mentioned the waxworks.

'What's ticklin' you, maister?' I said.

'Thoughts,' he says.

'What was you thinkin' about. Zummin funny, by the look aw't.'

'Well, 'twas funny in a way, although I did'n think 'twas very funny at the time. But I've auf'n laafed about it since. 'Twas you telling about waxworks that brought it back to me mind. You did'n know I was a waxworks wance, did 'ee?'

'You was a waxworks?'

'Ees. I'll tell 'ee all about it. I'm gwain back a long way, mind, 'cus I was only a young feller at the time. Well, the Boer War was on, then, so that'll tell 'ee. And 'twas everybody's talk, 'cus us had'n had so much experience of wars, tho, as what us have now. Us thought there never was sitch a war as that one, and never wude be again.

'In they days us used to get what they called Wuggett's Waxworks.'

'I remember Wuggett's Waxworks,' says Ned Annaferd. 'They used to come to Barleycombe rigler wance a year. They alwis sticked up a bill on our double doors and let us have a free ticket to go in vor nothin'. You mind Wuggett's Waxworks, Jan?'

'Of coorse, I do,' I says, 'as long as I can mind aught.' And sevver'l more o' the older ones said they cude mind it very well.

'But us never yers of it now,' I says. 'It died out years agone.'

'That's right,' says Silas. 'I dunnaw whe'er I had aught to do with its dyin' out or no, but I shude'n be at all surprised. What I be tellin' about now happened bevore I come thees way to live. I

27

was livin' then to a plaace called Braydown, about o' vower mile from Gurt Raxun.

'Well, and wan day a chap come around and sticked up the bills to zay that Wuggett's Waxworks was comin' to Raxun. That was alwis a big attraction, 'cus there was no sitch thing as the picshers, and so many other ole kickshaws, like there is now. But this time they had zummin extry speshul, a waxworks of Ole Krujer, the laider o' the Boers. I mind the wordin' now, in gurt letters as long as yer thumb:

'"A lifelike working vigger of President Krujer, zeed vor the fus' time in this country and patronised by royalty. Come and zee Krujer salute the Burtish flag."

'You must understand, the war was jist at its heighth at the time and everybody was mazed to go and zee ole Krujer. They started savin' up their happences soon's ever they knowed the waxworks was comin'. They reckoned 'twude be worth payin' money to zee ole Krujer salute the Burtish flag, 'cus jist about that time things wad'n gwain too well out there to Ostrillia.'

'Africay, you mean, Silas.'

'Africay, was it, Ned? Somewhere round they parts, I know. Be that as it may, everybody was tellin' every other body they was gwain to zee ole Krujer. Of a Mondy night, I remember, the show was, and that zame mornin' they all passed down by our plaace on the way to Raxun. Dree gurt waggins they had, and jist as they was gwain down over that steepy bit by Braydown the front waggin overrinned the hoss, they cude'n hold 'n back, the off wheels went up on the bank and over he goes; and the poor feller what was drivin' aw 'n had his leg broke off like a carrot. I yer'd the racket, where I was to brexis and rished out, and there the feller was, lied in the rawd with his leg broke. They carr'd'n into our plaace, and I sent off our chap fer Docter Jordan.

'Mr. Wuggett, the haid boss o' the waxworks, was wild as a hawk. But it wad'n the poor chap he was troublin' about. All that was worrittin' he was how he was gwain to manage without 'n.

'"I was one short bevore," he says, "and now I dunnaw how I be gwain to get thik hoss to Raxun. If the darn fule wanted to break his leg, why fer gudeness saake cude'n he wait till the end o' the journey?"

'I thought that was rather uncalled vor, 'cus I don't suppose the feller done it for his awn amusement. However, as I wad'n pa'ticler busy at the time, I offered to take on the hoss and waggin to Raxin vor vive shullins,and Mr. Wuggetts agreed to pay it. When us got to the plaace, he beggid of me to bide on fer a bit and assist'n to unload the dummies and fix up the show, 'cus he was so short-'anded and wude'n be ready in time, else.

'So us got to work and carr'd all they gurt boxes with the dummies inzide into the Town 'All. 'Twas a turk of a job, I can tell 'ee, haivin' 'em all up over the flight o' staps, but us got 'em all een, to-last, and then the viggers had got to be tooked out and sticked up in their proper plaaces. The conversation that went on while us was doin' that was nuff to make a cat laaf.

'"George, what have 'ee done with Quane Victoria?"

'"Her's behind the door, boss. You'll have to stick her up someplace where the volks can't see the back of her, 'cus that gurt rip in her dress id'n mended."

'"Well, where's Quane 'Lizabeth to?"

'"Her left leg's come off again. Sam's stickin' it on a minute."

'"Trig up the Juke o' Wellin'ton a bit, he's loppin' all over one zide, and putt Zur Francis Drake's 'at on straight. Have a clath, presen'ly, Sam, and wipe off King Alfred's faace. There's a lot o' black on his nawse. Better shove Boneypart back a bit, George, and putt Lord Roberts oppozyte the winder. Putt Shakespeare's hand up a bit more; he's supposed to be thinkin, not pickin' his teeth. And don't let 'n zit right in front o' Charley Peace like that. People wude rather zee a mudderer than a poet, any day."

'The last vigger of all to be trigged up was ole Krujer. A very speshul plaace was left vor he, 'cus that was the one all the volks was comin' to zee. He was to be putt right up in the middle o' the platvorm, and close to the front, where everybody cude have a gude view of 'n. Us was all warned to be most pa'ticler about ole Kruger, and us han'led him as if he'd bin our own mother. And I'm jiggered if he did'n look zac'ly like life itzell. There he was, sot in a cheer with his left hand rested on a li'l taable as natteral as cude be. A li'l ways off was the Burtish flag on a long stick; and every wipswile ole Kruger wude turn his haid towards the flag, raise up his right hand and salute 'n. Wonderful, 'twas. O' coorse he'd got clockwork in his innerds. But they tried 'n a time or two and he done it all splendid.

29

And then, you knows how it is. The very thing you'm tryin' to be most careful about is the very one you'm unlucky with. And 'twas so in thees caase. What happened egsac'ly I can't tell 'ee, but I consider Sam must have 'itched his voot in the leg o' the taable and pushed it up agin the president. Whether or no, all of a sudden us zee'd the ole feller topple vore, and bevore anybody cude move to zave 'en he went down wop on the floor from the whole heighth o' the platvorm. Bang on his haid he went, a proper buster.

'Us was all strick dummy fer a minute with the shock, and when us rished vore and turned over the poor ole chap, I'm beggered if he wad'n a pitiful zight to zee. His haid was scat all abroad and his brains knacked out; or they wude 'a-bin if he'd had any. One zide of his faace was in a hawful mess, and the eye clane gone. There was a hole you cude putt her vist in. He wad'n what you'd call a hanzum-lookin' chap to start wai', but now the last li'l bit o' buty was hat right out o'n. Dead as mutton, poor old Krujer was, there was no two ways about that.

'You never zee'd anybody zo cut-up as what Mr. Wuggetts was. If it had bin his awn brother, he cude'n 'a-bin more upzot. He was like anybody mazed, and the things he said I wude'n repait vor all the money in the world. I did'n matter that very much till he started sayin' 'em to me.

"'Old 'ard, guv'ner," I said. "You go and make they remarks to yer awn chaps. You daun' pay me vor that."

'But he still went on sayin' 'em to me, so to-last I said, "Look yer, mister, I know you've had a turrable bereavement in the vam'ly, and therefore allowance must be made, but if you zay any more o' them things to me, I shall give you such a tack in the yer-ole that yer awn brother won't be able to tell which is you and which is Krujer."

'That caused 'n to slow up a bit, and then he started to cry fer a change.

"'What shall I do?" he says. 'What shall I do? My butiful Krujer, which have bin advertised all over the place and which all the volks was comin' to zee!"

"'I'll tell 'e what," I said. "He've lost wan eye; knack off wan arm and call 'n Nelson."

"'I've done that already with Julius Sayzer," he says. "Us can't do with two Nelsons."

"'Well, cut off his haid and call 'n King Charles."

"'That won't give me back my Krujer, will it? If the volks can't zee Krujer they'll demand their money back."

'"They will in Raxun," I said. "And they'll zee they gets it, too. Nothin' won't plaise 'em better than to have a gude look to the other images vor nothin'."

'That set 'n off cryin' again, wiss 'n ever.

'"I tell 'ee what to do, boss," says George. "Stick wiskers on Mr. Gladstone and dress 'n up as Krujer. They won't know the differ'nce, and tid'n likely they'll miss Gladstone vor wan night."

'"And if they do," I said, "you can tell 'em he've jus' flipped across to the Rid Lion vor a drink. 'Twill zeem nice and natteral."

'But Mr. Wuggetts wude'n be cheered up.

'"What's the gude o' that?" he shouts. "Mr. Gladstone ab'm got a clock-work inzide, have he? Us ab'm got another model what cude salute the flag, and that's Krujer's gurt act."

'"Ees," I says. "That's what the volks be comin' to zee. If ole Krujer don't salute the flag they'll tear 'n limb from limb; and you too."

'Then he cried zome more.

'All to-once he jumped to me as if the dog had bit 'n.

'"I've got it," he says. "You must be Krujer."

'"You've got it all right, mister," I said. "But you'd better let it go again."

'"Us can dress 'ee up and stick wiskers on 'ee," he goes on, "and they'll never know the differ'nce if you'm careful."

'"Who, me?" I says.

'"Yas, you."

'"Not likely. You try that on one o' yer awn chaps. They'm a lot more resembling Krujer than what I be."

'"They can't be spared. They've got their awn jobs which must be 'tended to. But you cude do it aisy. 'Tis only to bide still and putt up yer hand every now and again."

'"Nothin' doin, maister," I says.

'"I'll give 'ee half-a-suvrin vor the night's work."

'"I cude'n come it," I says. "I was never a waxwork in me life."

'"'Tis ten shullins," says George.

'"'Tis a lot o' money," I said. "But I tell 'ee I cude'n indure it."

'"I'll make it a quid," says Wuggetts. "'Tis eether that or shut up the show."

31

'I was jus' gwain to refuse again when George lookid up to the ceilin' and said, "That's eighty pints."

'"Tell me what it is I've got to do," I said.'

'So you thought you cude be Krujer vor eighty pints, then, Silas?' says Ned Annaferd.

'I'd have bin the weather-cock on the church steeple vor that,' says Silas.

'And I suppose you drinked 'em all, fust and last?'

'Not I did'n, maister. I never drinked one of 'em. What's think o' that, now?'

'What did 'ee do, then; putt it into the bank?'

'I did'n putt it into the bank, ner I did'n buy a farm with it. I never even sot me eyes on it, never mind about me vingers.'

'What do 'ee mean? You never had it?'

'Never had a penny aw't, and never shan't in this world. And I hope I shan't get it in the next, 'cus I don't want to go where Wuggetts has gone to.'

'Is 'er daid, then, Silas?' axed Tom Zalter.

'I consider he is, Tom, although I've never zee'd head ner hair aw'n from that day to thees. But I shude zay he did'n live very long arter thik night. I reckon he died of apple-plexy.'

'Aw! You upzot 'n then, did 'ee?'

'He upzot hiszell, maister. I never zee'd anybody so upzot in all my live. I zee'd Farmer Urferd when Jan Grant's bullicks was in his young corn; I zee'd Mark Spiller when zomebody had drinked all his beer to the sheepshearing; I zee'd Tom Honeyset when he vound he'd bought back his own hoss again from the gipsies; and I was there on the spot when Poll Bradferd ketched her ole man takin' Jinny Sprigs to the wile-baiste show. But all they vower putt together wad'n the aiqual to Mr. Wuggetts when I lef' 'n last.'

'What happened then, Silas?'

'Nothin' but what anybody might expect from a human man. I tell 'ee, if you wants to be a waxworks you mus' be born a waxworks, not flesh and blid. In the fus' place they had to docter me up to look like Krujer, and that's no aisy job when you've got a hanzum-lookin' chap like me to start wai'.

'Fust of all they plastered my faace all over with zome bais'ly ole trade to look as if 'twas made o' wax. When that got properly set I veeled like as if I'd valled in the mud and then dried hard in the zin. My faace was all caked up like the bacon-dish arter the brekfus has got cold. When I tried to work it about to free it a bit, old Wuggetts went for me like a pick-pocket. "Not do that, stoobid," he says, 'Do 'ee want to get cracks all over yer faitures?"

"'Do you mean to zay," I says, "that I've got to keep my faace still from now till bimbye-a-night?"

"'Certinly you have," he says. "Waxworks don't keep on wrigglin' their faace about, and waxworks don't talk, nuther."

"'I don't care what waxworks does," I says, "but if you think I be gwain all they howers wai-out spaikin' there's a-plenty cude tell 'ee differ'nt. What do 'ee think I be gwain to do all that time?"

"'You mus' think about they eighty pints," says George.

'So I went thinkin' about the pints, and let 'em get on with the paintin' and decoratin'. They coloured me up accordin' to their fancy, and then they started stickin' a paacel of hoss-hair about me faace and neck. I'm beggered if that did'n cap the lot. I tried to get 'em to laive out the wiskers part and tell the volks 'twas Krujer in his courtin' days, bevore he gived up shavin'. But they wude'n knack off a single hair. There was'n the feelin's of a polecat amongs' the lot of 'em. They said the volks had all zee'd Krujer's image on the papers, and they'd reckon they'd bin chaited if they did'n get wiskers and all. That meant gubbin' up my faace with a lot of tacky ole trade, and when they'd done stickin' on the hoss-hair 'twas zac'ly like as if vorty thousand flays was havin' a precession in under me chin and around me neck.

"'I shall never be able to suffer it," I says, "and if I muzzen spaik 'tis cruelty to dumb animals. I wants to tear mezell in pieces, now this very minute."

"'You've got nice time to get use to that bevore the people starts comin' in," says Wuggetts. "You'll ferget all about it by then."

"'I shall never ferget it," I says, "if I lives to be as old as Methusalum."

'But I must zay, when I lookid at mezell in the lookin' glass I thought they'd made a wonderful job aw't. Darn if I wad'n zac'ly like the ole dummy.

"'Will this bais'ly stuff ever come off again?" I said. I had visions o' mezell gwain about like that to the end o' me days, and that meant sayin' Gude-bye to Nellie Ammitt. I'd got job enough as 'twas to keep her from lookin' at Joe Widlake, and this wude just about settle it.

'"Come off, ees!" says Wuggetts. "I'll let 'ee have the proper stuff bimbye. 'Twill get all that off as aisy as winky."

'Then they made me larn me actions. I had to zit down bezide the taable while the chap went around behind and made wise to wind me up. Then I had to turn me haid a bit jerkified, as if I'd got works inzide, lift up me hand and salute to the flag. I was glad I had they movements to perform, 'cus it give me a chance to do a bit o' scratchin' with me chin on me coller. But even then, I had to think hard about they eighty pints. Arter I'd bin droo they antics about a dizzen times they reckoned I was perfec'. Old Wuggetts got quite perky again, and George said I was a better dummy than the rale one.

'"If you keeps yer mind on what you'm doin'," they said, "and not go itemmin' about, the volks will never mistrust but what you'm the rale Krujer."

'"I hope to gudeness they won't," I thought to mezell. "If ever they surmises that I be Silas Wonnacott I shan't require no proper stuff to get me wiskers off. I shall be lucky if I've got any hair left 'pon tap of my haid, never mind about in under my chin."

'You know, there's a lot o' volks what don't like being had. Speshly when they've paid money vor it.

'When the time come, and they opened the door, the people properly straimed in, and I started shakin' in me shoes. I thought fer certin they must zee in a instant that I was only a rale man and not a dummy. But they did'n suspec' nothin'. 'Twas lucky vor me I was right up the far end o' the rume, so they had a lot o' statutes to pass bevore they come to me. That give me a little time to get me breath, as you might zay. But 'twas Krujer they'd come to zee most, and I very zoon had a crowd in front o' me. So then Wuggetts stood up and made a bit of a spaich like he did to all the viggers.

'"Yer you have the famous President Krujer," he says, "laider o' the Boers who be vightin' agin our boyes in Zouth Africay. You will now have the plaisure of zeein' him zalute the Burtish flag. Wind him up, George."

'George went around behind and pretended to do the windin' up, and then I started to go droo my capers. I'm jiggered if they wad'n all properly desayved. I had a hawful job to keep from bustin' out laafin' to yer the differ'nt remarks.

'"Look, mother, he'm movin'." "Caw, daun' it look rale?" "Anybody wude think he was alive, wude'n 'um?" "He opens and

shuts his eyes, lookee," "Now he's gwain to salute. Zee his hand
comin' up? There, zee! Id'n it marvellous?"

'And when I done me salute they all clapped like billy-o. I was
proper delighted with mezell. "Now I've done it once," I thought
to mezell, "I daun' care a button." So I went droo me prevor-
mance again, and the volks all gappin' with their eyes jumpin'
out o' their haids. Arter they'd had a gude look to me, Wuggettts
tooked 'em on to view Lord Roberts, and very thankful I was,
too. But I very nearly made a mess aw't, begad. Soon's they
turned their backs I was jis' gwain to have a stretch and scratch
mezell. That wude have bust the whole contrac', 'cus, o' coorse,
zome aw'm had stayed behind to zee me do it again. Speshly the
chillern, the li'l nuisances. I only jis' stapped mezell in time. And
then I'm bothered if I did'n go and stap altogether. I fergot to go
on with the haid-turnin' and salutin', and sevver'l stood their
waitin' vor it.

'"Caw," I thought to mezell, "what do I do now? I've give
mezell away." But blest if one o' they chillern did'n help me out,
nice.

'"Aw, look at that," her says. "He've rinned down." And then
her said to George, "Wind 'en up again, mister."

'But George done the right thing vor once. "Not jis' yet, my
dear," he says. "When the nex' lot comes around, then I will."

'That was a vine idaya, 'cus it give me plenty o' rest in
between. And when the volks zee'd I wad'n gwain to work again
vor a bit, they went off to view the other viggers. But I cude'n
move, ner scratch mezell, 'cus odd ones was all the time comin'
along to gappy to me, and 'twas amusin' to yer the differ'nt
remarks.

'"Id'n it rale," wan body said. "You can almost fancy 'tis
braithing."

'"'Tis braithe or bust," I said to mezell.

'One ole wumman said, "My, id'n he hugly? I never zee'd sitch
hugly faace."

'I had all the works in the world to keep from tellin' her to go
and look in the glass.

'However, everyting went on purty middlin', excep' that I was
achin' in all me bones from sittin' so long, when all of a sudden
who shude I zee comin' along but Joe Widlake with Nell Ammitt
hanged on his arm. Now, I regarded Nell as my maid, although

nothin' hadn't been settled, and I had a bit of suspicion that Joe was after her. And then to zee 'em come strollin' up like this, arm-an'-crook, made me go preckles all auver. The last crowd had jis' passed on, and when they two come up to me they was the only ones. And when they got close I zee'd that not only was they ketched hold arms, but they'd got their vingers all twined up together. Laur, massey, I cude veel even me hoss-hair wiskers standin' out straight.

'And bless yer zaul, to make matters wiss, they tooked a casual glimpse to me, and then turned their backs and sot down on the edge o' the platvorm. That's all they'd come to the waxworks vor. They did'n want to zee no dummies. All they wanted was to hold hands and wisper to wan tother. I moved me haid the slightest bit and lookid down, and there was the nearest part of Joe right in front of my voot. Just in aisy reach. I bust out all over into sw'attin'. I said to mezell, "Don't make yerzell a fule. Let it go till zome other time." Then I tried to think about eighty pints. I thought of 'em all-to-once, and one to a time. I picshered 'em all stretched out in a straight line and I picshered 'em all stood up in a heap. I thought of 'em all the ways I cude to try and take my mind off the couple sot right at me veet. But 'twas hard. And presen'ly I zee'd Joe let go to Nell's arm and putt his around her waist. And then 'twad'n hard; 'twas impossible. I drayed back me right voot and I let Mr. Joe have one kick that made 'n jump a yard high.

'O' coorse, by the time he turned around I was got straight again, and he cude'n think vor the life of 'n what had happened. But it done me gude to zee 'en rubbin' the place where it happened to. Then, I'm beggered if he did'n turn round and zit down again.

'"Well, I'm blest," I said to mezell, "you takes a lot o' convincin'." So I let 'n have another in the zame place, jis' vor luck. You never zee'd anybody's faace so full o' surprise and things as what Joe's was. But Nellie had noticed my voot move this time, and her went white as a sheet. Her ketched hold to Joe. "Joe," her says, "'tis alive."

'"Git-out with 'ee, alive," he says.

'"'Tis, Joe. I zee'd it move."

'"I'll soon let 'ee zee whether 'tis alive or not," he said, and started veelin' around the corner of his weskit, to zee vor a pin.

He'd got one, too; a darn gurt toad more like a stockin' needle. He reached 'n out towards my leg. I clinched me teeth, determined to stand the pain without flinkin' if I cude. But I might jis' as well think I was gwain to stand in front of a train without movin'. I'll bet he pushed thik pin a ninch into my leg. I give one yell, and I jumped clane off the platvorm on to Joe's chest. He went down like a strip o' paper, me with 'n, and bevore you cude count one, or even half a one, you cude'n tell which was Joe and which was me.

Nellie was scraimin' the place down, and there was uproar direc'ly. They got me and Joe apart, and then ole man Wuggetts and George took me on each end and sent me flyin' down over the steps like a bag o' meal. I did'n stap, ner I didn't even slow up, not till I got to the bottom. Then I thought about rishin' back and explainin' it all to Nellie. But by this time the people was comin' down the steps all aiger to go on where Wuggetts and George had laived off to. So, I thought again, and this time I started off 'ome, quicker than I ever did bevore, with half the neighbour'ude behind me. But 'twas dark and I bate 'em aisy.

'You did'n stop vor yer suvrin, then, Silas?'

'I did'n stop vor me suvrin, Ned, nor 'eet vor me vive shullins vor drivin' the hoss to Raxun. But wist o' the lot I did'n stop vor the stuff to get the varnish off my faace, and 'twas more 'n a wik bevore I cude show my nose outzide the door.'

JAN PLAYS GOLF

1. SEEING HOW IT IS DONE

They tell me zome people takes years to larn the way to play
golf. All I can zay is, I thought I was middlin' thick-'aided, but
I'm jiggered if it took me years, ner yet months. Not even wiks.
Two days is all I had; wan day watchin' others at it, and wan
day others watchin' me. And that's how long it took me to pick
up all I knaws about golf and all I wants to knaw. Two days; and
I've larned sufficient to last me a lifetime.

Tommy Bamfield was the wan what beguiled me into it. I
alwis use to look upon Tommy as a friend o' mine, but I shan't
never trust'n no more. I shan't never trust nobody what gives
their mind to golf, 'cus 'tis the most desatefullest, diddlin' paacel
of jiggery-pokery that was ever invented.

I'll tell 'ee all about it.

Mr. Bamfield is the ocshineer auver to Barleycombe. He's
properly mazed about this-yer golf caper, and he was everlastin'
keepin' on to me to go with 'n and try me hand to it. I kep'
saying p'raps I wude when I had the time to spare, so wan day
he said:

'Jan,' he says, 'I be comin' to call for you nex' Zaturdy in my
motor to take 'ee to the golf.'

'So do,' I said, I wad'n so very anxious about the golf part,
but I thought if he mind to take me fer a nice ride, us wude'n
vall out about that.

When I went 'ome and told my Ann about it her was most
mortle excited.

'You'll be auver there amongs' all the bettermost volk to
Barleycombe,' her said. ''Tis something fer Mr. Bamfield to pick
on you like that. He've never took no other body from Muddlecombe village to the golf bevore, seps Dr. Jinkins and Squire

Porter. They'm the only two in this parish what goes to the golf, so you ought to think yerzel' 'ighly 'onnered.'

Ees, and durin' the nex' vew days I'm beggered if her did'n manage to let every other wumman in the village have the news. Did'n matter what subjic' they was on upon, her'd scheme it around zome-'ow to fit it in that her ole man was gwain off with the gen'lvolks to Barleycombe to take part in the golf.

O' coorse, her had'n got no more idaya what it was to do than what I had. All her trouble was, what clothes I ought to wear.

'You daun't want to go there lookin' like a gawk,' her says, 'and let 'em think you dunnaw all about it.'

'I daun't zee why I shude want to stap 'em from thinkin' the truth,' I says. 'I daun't knaw the fust thing about it, never mind *all* about it.'

But that did'n satisfy mother. Her reckoned I had'n got nuff self-pride.

'There's sure to be proper clothes to wear for the purpose,' her says, 'same's there is with cricket and vootbaal. I'd sooner you spend a vew shullin's and went auver there lookin' proper vitty than to go shawin' yer ignerance and makin' a table-talk. I'll ax Mr. Annaferd. He reads the paapers a lot, and very likely he cude tell a body.'

So nex' time her zee'd Ned go past the houze her called 'n een and putt matter to 'en.

'Well, missis,' says Ned, 'I dunnaw that I can tell 'ee very much, but from what I can make out, they gener'ly wears what they calls plush-vowers.'

'That's right,' says Ann. 'Now you come to mention it, I've yer'd 'em tell about they plush-vowers. What be 'um like, Mr. Annaferd?'

'That I can't tell 'ee, missis.''

'I wonder where I cude vind out,' her says. 'I've got they ole plush curtins upstairs which us never uses. There's vower o' thay, so 'twude be jis' right. If I cude get the pattern I dersay I cude run 'em up with the machine.'

'No, you waun't do nothin' o' the sort,' I says. 'If you thinks I be gwain auver there trigged out in plush curtins you'd better think again, and think zummat differ'nt.'

'Daun' be so stoobid,' says mother. 'Who's gwain to know they was curtins? They'm the very best plush that money can

buy. They'm hardly faded a bit, and see the years they hanged up
to the winders.'

'Well, you can hang 'em up there again,' I says. 'You ban't
gwain to hang 'em on me, so I tell 'ee straight.'

But mother cude'n let it rest, and bothered if her did'n go right
away up to Tilda Grinnaway, the dressmaker, to zee if her cude
tell her aught about plush-vowers. Tilda went rummagin'
amongs' a heap o' they fashin bukes and furridged out wan with
a picsher of a chap in this-yer rig-out. Vine job that was, and
mother come rinning home with 'n, to show me what I ought to
look like. You never zee'd sitch a sight in your life. 'Twas nothin'
more ner less than a gash'ly-lookin' pair o' burches about ten
sizes too big. They looked fer all the gude in the world like a
couple o' rag-bags with holes in the bottom vor the veet to poke
out.

'I cude make a pair like that,' her says.

'Yas, and you can wear 'em, too,' I says. 'I daun' doubt fer wan
minute but what you cude make 'em. But not vor me.'

'Daun' be so sauft. I want to send 'ee auver there dressed
proper.'

'That's right, mother. But if I was to wear they thiings I shude
consider I was dressed improper. So daun' 'ee zay no more
about it. There's gwain to be no plush-vowers vor me. I'll wait till
I be zick and tired o' life and then I'll have a pair of plush-eights
and go out and drown mezelf in 'em.'

So I weared the same togs as what I wude if I was gwain into
Ex'ter, and when I got to the plaace I found I wad'n no differ'nt to
the rest. I did zee a couple o' chaps with they rag-bags on, but
they wad'n plush. Only ordnery clath.

Mr. Bamfield come to call fer me with his moter, same's he said
he wude, and drived me to the golf plaace. I'd bin thinkin'
matters auver, and I'd made up me mind I wude'n take no part in
it, fust go off, but only watch the rest and get a bit of idaya what
'twas like. Then I shude'n be so likely to make a fule o' mezell
when it come to my turn. I told Tommy that, gwain in-along. I
thought p'r'aps he'd be a bit upzot, but he wad'n.

'If you think you'd rather do that, Jan,' he says, '"twill suit me
better. Matter o' fact,' he says, 'I met with a gen'lman 's-mornin'
from up-the-country who's suppaused to take a middlin' gude
hand to it, and as I be considered wan o' the best in our club, he

beggid o' me to give'n a game, and 'tis the only chance us have got. But I cude aisy vind zomebody to have a round with you, so's you shan't be disappointed.'

'No disappointing about it, Mr. Bamfield, I'd sooner look on at you two, if you daun' objec'.'

'I dunnaw but what 'twude'n be all-so-well, Jan,' he says. 'You'd be able to get zome idaya o' the game bevore you venter on it.'

So that's what I done, and I got idaya o' the game all right. But 'twad'n hardly the idaya he reckoned I was gwain to get.

I'll explain in a minute what they two fellers done, and then you shall tell me if 'twad'n more like a couple o' skule chillern itemmin' about than two middle-age men.

Fust of all us went in what they calls the club-'ouze. That's a vine swell plaace with butiful aisy cheers sticked about. I wondered to zee so many aisy cheers till I'd vinished me day's golf, and then I vound the raison vor 'em. I'm darned if a feller can't do with a aisy cheer arter wan gude go at that caper. I shude be vor taking wan along with me.

I alwis thought they played in a vield. Laur bless yer zaul, they can't do with a vield; they wants a distric'. Wance you've started out, you'm zummin like the chap what went seekin' fer the North Pole; you never knaws when you'll be comin' back again.

My dear days, it only shows what amount o' trouble and bother zome volks will go to so long as you don't call it work. If they two fellers had bin made to trapes all they miles and go droo such a paasel of manoovers just to plaise zome other body, what a fuss they wude 'a-made. They'd have played Amlick, I'll warran' they wude. If they was forced to do it in the ordnery way o' business they'd consider they was the hardest done by of any volks on the face o' the earth.

The other gen'lman was there waitin' in the club-'ouze, and very nice he was, too, before he started on with the golf, and then I'm jiggered if he wad'n a proper nuisance. Well, they'm all the zame, come to that. They waun' spaik a word about nothin' else. You can't yer nothin' but 'andy-caps, and foozlums, and bunkums, and mashers and nibble-its, and putts and chips, and how many strokes they can make to the hour or the mile, I ban't sure which. If you mentions anybody's name to try and change the subjic', all they zay is, 'What's his 'andy-cap?'

41

And their tays. They keeped on tellin' about tay, and I tell 'ee straight I cude 'a-done with a dish o' tay very well. But it all ended with talk. I did'n zee no zign o' tay, ner nothin' else. I'd 'a-gived a shullin and welcome vor a pint o' zider. Bevore us had gone half the journey I cude'n spit a zixpence. Yet every now and again they'd bring up about the tay, which only made it wiss.

And then, whatever do you think they come to talkin' about next? When they cude'n think o' nort else nonsensical they started tellin' about bogies. Bogies, mind 'ee! Two grawed up men yappin' about bogies. If it had a-bin pixies it wude'n 'a-bin so bad. But when they started on about bogies I thought to mezell, 'It only shows 'ee what a state o' mind golf can bring anybody to.'

But laur, what else can you expec' when you come to witness the game? When us was in readiness to start they tooked a bagful o' sticks apiece and marched off.

Us stopped when us come to a bit of a flat plaace and they both chucked their bags down on the ground. But each aw'm tooked out wan stick with a nob on the end. And that's when they started makin' sillies o' theirzel's.

Fust of all the gen'lman went to a li'l box and tooked out a han'ful o' durt. And what do you suppause he done wai' 't? He stoopied down and made a li'l heap on the ground. I thought he was tryin' to be funny jis' to make us laaf, but I zee'd Tommy Bamfield wad'n gwain to laaf, so I took it to be that the poor feller was a bit tiched up under the roof, as the sayin' is. Natcherly, I veeled sorry vor 'en. But when he fished out a li'l white ball and sticked he up on tap o' the heap o' durt, I thought I shude 'a-bust out.

And then if you'd zee'd the antics he went droo arter that, I'll make a bet you'd 'a-roared. He went and stood bezide this-yer ball with the stick in his hand, spraid out his veet and started aimin' at the ball with the nob on the end o' the stick. About a dizzen times he aimed at 'n as if he was promisin' what he'd do to 'en if he did'n behave hiszell. Then he stopped and lookid all around to zee if anybody was watchin aw 'n. And I daun' wonder at it, nuther. He wude'n wish fer any stranger to zee 'en make sitch a fule of hiszell, for certin. Then he aimed to the ball again a time or two and I thought to mezell, 'Now he's gwain to knack 'n.'

But no. He stapped back away from the ball and started swishin' his stick around, knackin' off bits o' grass. Then he come back to the ball again and lookid at 'n, as gude as to zay, 'How fer gudeness sake did you get there?'

Then he started itchin' his veet as if he was squaishin' a black-biddle. Next he beginned to wriggle his body, like a chap with a flay in the middle of his back where he can't scratch 'n. Then all-to-once, he up with his stick and he fetched thik poor li'l ball sitch a clout, and hat 'n so-fur as he cude zee 'en. Wonder to me he did'n knack the inzide right out aw'n.

'Caw!' I thought to mezell, 'that's the end o' that wan, fer certin. Do he get a cigar for that, I wonder, or a nit?'

Well, and then I'm blawed if Tommy did'n go droo precisely the zame antics, and he hat a ball likewise. Then they both picked up their bags and walked off.

'Have us got to go and vind they balls?' I said.

'Certin'ly,' says Tommy. 'What do 'ee think?'

'I think,' I says, 'that if you did'n whack 'em hardly so hard us wude vind 'em a lot more aisy.'

However, us found 'em all right, and then I'm jiggered if they did'n take another stick apiece, and fetch they balls another whack. Then us had to trapes arter 'em again. Well, I was beginnin' to get a bit weary of walkin' about lookin' fer balls, so I said:

'How many times do you reckon you'm gwain to do this bevore you begins to play?'

Then I found they was playin', if you plaise. This was part of it.

Arter they'd give the balls another scat or two, us come to a nice flat bit o' grass with a hole in the middle about the size of a quart pot, and they both truckled their balls into the hole.

'Is that the finish?' I said to Tommy.

'No, ti-no. That's the fust hole. Us goes on to the second, now.'

And then, by Jo, they went droo the zame ole pantomine again. Li'l heap o' durt, ball on the tap, the stick with the nob on the end, squashin' the black-biddle, flay down the middle o' the back, then, Whack! Away goes the balls. Away goes we to vind 'em. Bim-by us come to another li'l hole in the grass, and they truckled in their balls again. From what I can make out, 'tis the wan what can get his ball into the hole fust.

Two mortle howers us went on like that, scattin' the balls as fur

43

as they'd go and then lookin' vor 'em. Us trapesed miles, and keeped on vindin' fresh li'l holes all auver the place. Zometimes wan o' they fellers wude scat his ball a bit ockerd and 'twude go off the track into the vuz or the brimmles. Then us might be there tain minutes or more seekin' vor 'n. You'd 'a-thought, sooner than waste all that time, they'd have a fresh ball. But if it had bin golden suvrins they cude'n be more keen to vind 'en. And what was the gude? When they *did* vind 'en they only whack 'n furder again.

And that's all 'twas, all the way droo the piece; whack, walk and look; whack, walk and look, and then dap it in a hole. You counts how many scats you gives 'en before he goes een, and the wan what gives the laistest number o' scats is the winner. I made out that much.

But I though to mezell, 'You tell about larnin' to play golf! What is there to larn, fer gudeness saake? Nort. Any fule cude do this. I wish I had'n said I wude'n take part,' I said to mezell. 'I'll make a bet I cude scat thik ball furder than eether-wan o' they cude. I'll bet a guinea I cude.'

Bim-by, arter us had trapesed half-ways round the world, us got back to club-'ouze, and Tommy said, 'What be gwain to have, Jan?'

'Twas the fus' sainsible remark he'd made since us started.

Tom reckoned he'd winned the golf by wan hole, and he'd had zempty-nine scats to the ball. He zimmed to consider that was very gude, and zo did the tother gen'lman, but I thought 'twas a doost of a lot, mezell.

'Caw, darn my rigs,' I thought, 'if I cude'n hat thik ball around that distance in less knocks that zempty-nine I'd ait the li'l toad, stick and all.'

'Twas too laate fer me to have a go at it then, so I promised I'd go auver again the volleyin' Zaturdy and have a game 'long o' Mr. Bamfield.

'I shall be yer waitin' vor 'ee, Jan,' he says. 'If you can manage to come auver on the bus, I'll drive 'ee home.'

2.   SHOWING HOW TO DO IT

I'll take back all I've said about the blimmin' ole golf. I wish to gudeness I cude take back the whole blessid thing, so's nobody

44

wude'n know nothin' about it. But 'tis too laate fer that. Wan o' these vine days I shall yer the last aw't, but 'twaun't be yet a bit, I'm 'fraid.

Where I made mistake to, I opened me mouthe a bit too soon and a lot too wide. Like a gude many else, I used me tongue fust, instaid o' keepin' aw'n till last. What I ought to have done, if I'd had any sainse, I ought to have held me noise till I'd bin droo the whole rigmarole, and then zay whatever I'd got to zay. I shude have bin tellin' about what I knowed, instaid of what I thought I knowed, which is a very differ'nt thing. Instaid o' tellin' the volks what I'd done, I went tellin' 'em what I was gwain to do, and that's a fule's way o' gwain to work. Never say too much about what you'm gwain to do, speshly if 'tis zummat you've never done bevore. If you do, ten to wan you'll make yerzell a laafin'-sport, same as zomebody have done that I cude mention by name.

Natcherly, when I got back from the golf everybody wanted to know what I thought about it. And like a gawk I told 'em.

"'Tis cheel's play,' I said, 'and you can't call it no other. Scattin' a li'l ball with a long stick and then gwain arter it, what else can you term that but cheel's play? And then they tells about larnin' to do it, as if there was aught to larn about it. If Tom Trott, there, was to let his li'l Jimmy have a walkin' stick and a door-nob, I cude larn 'en all there is to larn about golf in two minutes. They've got to get up to all manner o' redeclus antics, aimin', and measurin' and stiddin', and preparin' and luggin' about a gurt bag o' tools, jis' to pretend 'tis difficult, and make out they'm very clever. I'll make a bet I'd hat the ball furder than eether-wan aw'm, wai'out all thik ole pantomine.'

That's what I said, and a lot more bezides, becus if a chap ab'm got sainse nuff to knaw when to start that sort o' tomfulishness he won't have gumtion enough to knaw when to stop, that's fer certin.

When the time come fer me to go to the golf again, Ned Annaferd and Lias Buzzacott went along too. They axed me if they might, and I said they cude and welcome. When a feller starts makin' a fule of hiszell he gener'ly do's the thing proper. I was turrable plaised at the time that they shude come and zee me play golf.

I'd give vive pound now, if they cude 'a-bin hunderd mile away. If Ned and Lias had'n bin there to watch I might 'a-bin able to keep it dark. But from what I can zee aw't, they waun' be satisfied till everybody fer tain mile around have yeard how Jan Stewer played golf.

Mr. Bamfield was there, ready and waitin' when us got to the plaace, and he had his wive along with 'n.

'You daun' mind my missis comin' around, do 'ee, Jan?' he saith. 'Her ab'm played a lot, and I thought her'd be more about your mark, 'cus her's only larnin'.'

'Coorse, I said I was very plaised, and so I was, 'cus Mrs. Bamfield's a very nice laady. But all the zame, I thought 'twas like Tommy's chick to zay her'd be about my mark. I said to mezell, 'I'll let you zee all about my mark in a minute, ole Cock o' the Walk.' I winkid across to Ned, as gude as to zay, 'You 'old 'ard, and zee.' And ole Ned he nodded back, as much as to zay, 'I be lookin'.'

Tommy had his bag o' tools, and he'd fetched along another bagful fer me to lug about. I did'n zee no sainse in taking along that lot, 'cus they was a tidy heft, so I said one wude be sufficient vor me and I'd laive the rest behind. But he was very aiger that I shude take the lot, so I did'n make no more bones about it, speshly as Mrs. Bamfield had got a bagful to carr'.

Tommy said I mus' larn the names of all the sticks, and he tooked 'em out from the bag one to a time and showed 'em to me. I can't mind all their names now, but the chap with the big nob was the driver, and then there was a wan called a masher, and a nibble-it, and a putter. Quare lookin' sample they was, take 'em wan with another.

I'll tell 'ee what they did look like, fer all the gude in the world. They lookid like set o' weedin' tools fer the garden.

'Anybody wude think us was gwain cuttin' dashels,' I says.

I reckon zomebody must 'a-bin usin' 'em purty bad, 'cus they was twisted all shapes. Speshly the nibble-it feller. Properly out o' the straight he was. The hannle was all right, but the li'l hoe on the end was hawful crooked. I spause Tommy thought any ole thing wude do fer me, but I did'n complain about it, 'cus I reckoned I shude'n require to use more'n wan o' the tools.

When us got the startin' paust Mr. Bamfield said, 'Now, Jan, I be gwain to drive off, and you take pa'ticler notice how I do's it.'

And then I understood him to zay he was gwain to make tay.

'Bit early fer that, maister, id'n it?' I says. 'I've only recently had me dinner.'

46

Caw, did'n 'um laaf! Then I found that what he called makin' tay was heapin' up thik handful o' durt what I told 'ee about, to rest the ball on.

'You haves yer driver vor this stroke,' he says. So he tooked out the stick with the nob at the bottom, and then he started gwain droo all they ole crams again, pretendin' to get ready fer zummin wonderful, 'itchin' his veet, and wrigglin' his tail and swingin' his arms around to make sure they was in gear. Then he let rip to the ball and fetched 'n a turrable scat. Mind you, I will zay he sent 'n a doost of a way; but I considered I cude better it when it come to my turn.

Then Mrs. Bamfield had a go to it. Her went droo all the zame antics, but her did'n zend the ball much more 'n half the distance. Still, I had to zay that was very gude fer a laady, 'cus I did'n want vor her to get down-couraged.

'Now, Jan, you have a try,' says Tommy; and he let me have a ball to scat. 'Bout the size of a pullet's egg he was, only round, o' coorse. I putt 'n down on the floor.

'Better tay 'en up,' he says. 'I'll make a tay for 'ee.'

'No, let 'n bide as he is,' I says. 'I can hat 'n all-so-well there.'

I did'n mind scattin' a ball about to amuse 'em, but I wad'n gwain to play makin' mud pies to plaise nobody. And I thought to mezell, 'I ban't gwain droo no stoobid ole antics, nuther. You said I was to watch you, now you watch me.'

So I ups with me driver and I let go wan blow to thik ball which I considered wude scat 'n across dree parishes. In fac', I putt so much force behind 'n I swinged mezell right off me feet, 'cus I was determined to send the li'l toad to Jericho. Lias was stood zix voot behind me, but he only ducked his haid just in the nick o' time. Another second and I'd have scat out his brains with my stick.

'Where have that wan gone to?' I said, when I got back.

'He ab'm started yet,' says Tommy.

'What do 'ee mean, not started?'

Caw, I'm jiggered! When I come to look, there was the blessid ball, zac'ly where I putt 'n to. I had'n moved the li'l begger.

'Mean to zay I missed 'n?' I says.

'You did'n acsh'ly miss 'n, Jan,' says Ned. 'You hat 'n about a voot too high up.'

'Get on with 'ee,' I says. "Twad'n nothin' like that. Cude'n 'a-bin much more'n a hair's breath.'

'Try again, Jan,' says Tommy.

'Wait a miinute,' says Lias. 'Let me get behind a tree.'

'Don't go quite so hard this time,' says Tommy. But I reckoned I knawed what he was up to. He did'n want fer me to send my ball beyond he's; so I hat 'n a bit harder if anything. But I didn't have me stick hold hardly tight enough and he slipped right out of me hand. If Ned Annaferd had'n jumped up in the air smarter than he have fer the last vorty year, 'twude 'a-ketched he a wop in the leg. He'd have knawed which leg 'twas too, vor thikky stick flied a gun-shot bevore he valled to ground.

'Yer 'old 'ard, Jan,' he says. 'I thought you was playin' golf, not Aunt Zally.'

'I'm gwain to sit on the ball,' says Lias. 'That's the safest place, looks-so. Jan ab'm titched that wan.'

I'm bothered if it wad'n true, too. There the ball was, same's ever, lookin' up to me so innocent, as if he did'n know I'd ever had a stick in me 'and.

Mr. Bamfield said, 'You mus' keep yer eye on the ball, Jan.'

'I shude if I was you, Jan,' says Lias. 'You'll be sure it won't get hurted, there.'

'And you mus' keep yer haid still, likewise.'

'If Lias had kep' his still,' says Ned, 'he'd have had it knocked off by now.'

'Many worse things than that might hap'm,' I said, 'cus between you and me, I was gettin' a bit wopsy. I knowed very well 'twas only Mrs. Bamfield's gude manners was keepin' her from laafin' right out; and the same with Tommy. The other two had'n got no gude manners, and they was bustin' their sides.

'I zee what's the matter, Mr. Bamfield,' says Lias. 'You have'n gived Mr. Stewer a proper outfit. You've only let 'n have a driver. What he wants is a conducter as well.'

'He'd need to be a lightnin' conducter to keep out o' the way o' that stick,' says Ned.

However, I went and got me driver back again, and I let go to thik ball with a whack which shude have zend 'n to Halifax. But it did'n turn 'en auver. It did'n touch 'en. You wude'n believe it was possible, wude 'ee? But 'tis true as I'm sot yer. There was the ball, and there was a long stick with a gurt nob, and there was

me, and do you think I cud shift the little baiste? I swished at 'en
with all me might and he lied there laafin' at me. Then I lost me
temper and started swingin' me stick like the ole wumman baitin'
carpets. Zix goes I had, wan arter t'other, and I did'n make no more
differ'nce to the ball than if he wad'n there. But if Mrs. Bamfield
had'n been stood close handy I'd have called he somethin' that
wude have made 'n bury hiszell in the ground. I was bustin' to zay
it, and I *did* zay a bit of it. And then her laafed, manners or no
manners.

'You'd better putt'n up on a tay, Jan,' says Tommy. ''Tis proper
thing to do.'

So he putt down a handful o' durt and rised the ball up a bit. And
this time I hat 'n a buster. I knowed I had 'cus I yeard the crack.

'Did anybody zee where that wan went to?' I says, ''cus I did'n.'

'You wude'n be likely to,' says Lias, 'without you'd got eyes in
yer tail. If you stap back you'll putt yer voot on it.'

He was right. I turned around and there the ball was, not a tailor's
yard away; and the oppozyte derection to what he shude 'a-bin.
How do he do it, can anybody tell me?

'Better have that wan again,' says Tommy, and he trigged 'n up
on the tay wance more.

By this time I was beginnin' to wonder whether I was quite so
clever as I thought I was. I wished with all me 'art and zaul I had'n
had quite so much to zay about what I was gwain to do. I 'ope 'twill
be a lesson to me for the future.

'Let me show 'ee how to hold yer club, the right way,' says
Tommy. And I let 'n to, like a lamb. Vive minutes bevore I shude
have considered me awn way was best. But I'm jiggered if thik li'l
ball had'n took the stuffin' out o' me.

This time I did manage to knock 'n vore a bit, but 'twad'n half the
distance of Mrs. Bamfield's, let alone Tommy's.

'That's more like it,' he says. ''Tis in the right derection, anyway.
Bring yer bag along, and knock 'n a bit furder.'

So us walked to where my ball was lied on the grass, and Mr.
Bamfield said I must have wan o' the garden tools this time. I started
off back.

'Where be gwain?' he says.

'For a handful o' durt,' I said. 'I shall have a tay this time.'

But that id'n allowed in the rules, don't seem so. You can only
have a tay for the fust start off. Arter that you mus' knock the ball

wherever he lies to. And I can tell you, he lies in some very vunny places, zometimes. Mine did, anyway. 'Twude be redec'lus to zay a li'l white ball can think for hiszell and choose what place he shall creep into, but I'll make a bet, if there *was* a bit of a hole in the ground or any sort of ockerd place where he cude squaise in, he'd get in there, zome'ow. He was in wan now.

I dreads to tell 'ee what happened next. Tommy said I must have a go at 'n with the masher, so I did. Matter o' fact, I had vive goes at 'n, bevore ever I touched 'n at all, and when I did fetch 'n a scat, to-last, he did'n go a bit the way I was lookin'. He flied up in the air like a burd and come down in a pit full o' sand. And you try to knock a ball out of a heap o' sand with a crooked hoe and zee what 'tis like. I was for pickin' out the li'l toad and restin' him on the hard ground. But you muzzen do that, by all accounts. 'Where he lies to!' That's the rules.

'Well, then,' I said, 'they did'n ought to go leavin' ditches about like this. I shude think considerin' all the money they've spent on the place, they cude afford to fill this one in, and putt a bit o' turf auver it.'

My, did'n Tommy Bamfield laaf!

'That's putt there a-purpose,' he says, 'to make it more difficult.'

'I shude think 'tis plenty difficult enough,' I says, 'without any making.'

'Ullaw!' says Ned, 'I fancy zomebody have changed his chune. I understood 'twas cheel's play.'

'That's right,' I says. 'I've bin waitin' vor that. You come and have a try at it, and you'll do the same as I'm gwain to do.'

'What's that, then?'

'Why, tell a differ'nt tale,' I says.

I wude'n like to tell 'ee how many whacks I had to the ball bevore I got 'n out from the sand, nor how much o' the sand I shifted in the transaction. I'm thankful to zay the rest of 'em got a gudish bit of the sand down the backs o' their necks, and Lias got a mouthful, which made 'n ferget what he was gwain to zay.

I got my li'l joke out o' that lot, too. The very fust whack I give the ball, instaid of he coming out, as I ordained for 'en to, he went right in and buried hiszell. They all started to laaf, but I said: 'Well,' I said, 'there's wan thing I can zay. I *can* boast that I hat my ball right out o' sight, and that's more than eether of you can.'

Ned Annaferd said, 'I thought this golf you was doing, Jan, not badger-digging.'

They ditches be called 'bunkums' so I understand, and a very gude name for 'em, too. There's dizzens of 'em about, all auver the plaace, and I shude think, fust and last, I must have got in every wan of 'em at laist twice. Every time I hat a ball, I eetherways missed 'n altogether, or else he went flyin' off lookin' vor a bunkum. If he cude'n vind a bunkum he'd go down a rabbut-'awl, or else in a vuz-bush. If there'd been a hen's nest about I'll make a bet he'd have crept into that one and pretended he was a winedot's egg.

However, arter a vew more scats us come to the smooth grassen plat with the hole in the middle. That's what they calls a green, and you've got to make yer ball go in the li'l pot. If it had only been a hole where he wad'n suppaused to go, I cude have got mine in as aisy as winky. All I'd have to do wude be to shut me eyes and give 'n a scat, and in he'd go. But do you think he'd go in when I wanted vor 'en to? Not he wude'n. He'd go around 'en, or he'd jump auver the tap of 'en, or he'd go to the edge and keen down auver the side. He'd do any mortle thing, seps go een.

When I did get 'n in, to-last, they said I'd had zeb'm and twenty knocks for thik hole, from start to finish. Mrs. Bamfield had zeb'm and Tommy had vive.

Lias said they ought to reckon it the zame as they do cricket, and then I shude be the winner, aisy. Ned Annaferd was figgering with a pencil and a bit o' paaper.

'What's be you up to?' I said.

'I was jis' doin' a bit o' 'rithmetic,' he says. 'How many o' these-yer holes did you say there was, Mr. Bamfield?'

'Eighteen, Ned. But us waun't be able to do 'em all to-day. Us'll take a short cut.'

'That's eighteen times zeb'm-an'-twenty,' says Ned. 'Jan said las' wik you tooked zempty-nine, and he was gwain to show you the way to do it proper. As near as I can work it out, at the rate he've gone on already, 'twill take he vower hunderd and eighty-zix. So I propose he shude give us a wik's notice when he'm coming towards the last 'ole, and then us'll come auver and zee 'en finish.'

GINGER'S FORTUNE

There's heaps o' volks round about these parts who can mind Abdul the Prophet. Not the younger wans, 'cus he was finished up and gone bevore their time. But when I was a young feller, Abdul and his wive used to be to all the fairs and revels as rigler as clockwork, tellin' fortunes. And people used to putt a lot o' faith in 'en, too. I'll make a bet there's scores o' volks, even to this day, what cude tell 'ee of things that Abdul foretold which come true. They daun't tell 'ee o' the things which did'n come true, 'cus they waun't admit they was such fules as to be took in.

Abdul used to have a booth with 'orrible picshers painted all over the outzide; ghoasts, and witches, and black men, and rid devils with horns and long tails, and a lot more gashly things which nobody cude'n understand, but which gived 'ee the creeps bevore you went in. The Prophet was a long, skinny chap, with a gurt hook nawse, and he weared a sort of a long black gown with hugly faaces all over 'en, and a rid hat like a saaspan without a hannle. His missis was a gurt vat piece, in a rid dress with black cats on 'en, and a black mask to cover up half her faace. As far as looks was consarned, 'twude 'a-bin all-so-well if her'd covered up the other half.

The booth had a gurt curtin in place of a door, and Mrs. Abdul wude bide outzide and take people's money, and then keep 'em waiting till the prophet was ready. Her was artful nuff to get their money as they come along, but they cude only go in wan to a time so they had to wait vor their turn. If they had'n paid they wude'n have waited, and zometimes they had to bide there a hower or more, or else go away and lost their zixpence; that's if Abdul was doin' a gude trade and plenty o' maids wanted to knaw if there was a dark man coming vor 'em.

52

When it come to your turn, Mrs. Abdul wude lift up the curtin a bit and let 'ee into the nex' compartment where the prophet was. There was only a speezin' cannle-light in there, shinin' droo rid glass, makin' everything look gashly; and there was boans, and skulls and skelletons about whichever way you looked. So you was ready to believe anything you was told and only glad nuff to get out again alive.

I only went in there wance, when I was about nineteen or twainty. I did'n have very much of a fortune, 'cus I cude only afford zixpence, but I spause 'twas as much as anybody cude expect vor the money. I was gwain a journey, I remember, and a relation I'd never yeard of was gwain to die and lef' me zome money. 'Twad'n gwain to be a turrable lot, but if I'd paid a shullin I should have had a hannle to me name and married a rich wive. Vor half-a-crown I cude have been a lord or a juke with a gurt estaate and a thousand a year and a pound a wik.

However, 'tid'n mezelf I be gwain to tell 'ee about. 'Tis about Alfy Bidder.

Alfy was a young feller that lived in our parish and alwis went by the name o' Ginger, on account o' the colour of his hair. Ginger valled in love wai' a maid called Kate Maddaway. And when I zay he valled in love, I mean he done the thing proper. Valled in haid auver yers, he did. Mazed about her he was. He cude'n spaik about nothin' else, and he used to think about her all day and draime about her all night. He'd laive his work and rin a mile if he thought he was only gwain to glimpse her passin' by in the rawd. Aw, ees, he'd got it bad, there's no two ways about it.

The unforchnit part was, Kate did'n zeem to be zo vast about vallin' in love with Ginger as what he was with her. Matter o' fact, her was turrable slow about it. He done everything he cude think of to ketch her eye and try to make her take a vancy to 'en, but he did'n zeem to make very much haid-way.

Ginger knawed what the trouble was. Bert Yatton was the trouble. Bert was more likely to ketch a maiden's eye than what Alfy was. He was more 'ansum fer wan thing; there was no gettin' away from that. Very dark, Bert was, with black hair and black mustosh, and black eyes which properly zeemed to spark zometimes. Anybody wude be bound to take notice of Bert in a crowd, whereas Ginger wude be overlooked if he was stood by hiszelf, 'cus he was only ordnery, and not very much o' that. Short he was, too, and tooked a large size in butes, but Bert was a vine upstandin' chap, with small veet and hands like a lady.

And Bert had a way with the maidens. He cude alwis vind zummin to zay to please 'em, or make 'em laaf, where Ginger wude be stuck like a gawk and not be able to think o' nothin' till 'twas too laate. Very gude chap vor work, Ginger was. Worth two o' Bert Yatton, so-fur as that goes, but nothin' to look at and not very much to harken to.

Ginger veeled purty sure that if only Bert was out o' the way he wude'n have no trouble in gettin' Kate. He wad'n feared o' no other body. 'Twas only this ansum-lookin', dressed-up tailor's dummy that was keepin' her from regardin' him in a proper manner, and he used to spend howers, day and night, thinkin' and stiddin' what he cude do to alter it.

Well, and then come Muddelcombe Revel, which was alwis held of a Whit-Mondy. Everybody vor miles around used to come to Revel in our parish, and join in the murry-makin'. Kate Maddaway was there, and where Kate was, Bert and Alfy wad'n very fur behind. Matter o' fact, Bert wad'n behind at all. He was right up bezide. Ginger was a bit behind, as usual, 'cus he had'n got the gift fer that sort o' thing like Bert had. He wad'n no aiger to go spendin' money on fairin' and other trumpery as what tother feller was, and maidens likes a bit o' money spent on 'em at such kickshaws. Bert was takin' Kate around to everything. Took her to zee the vat wumman and the bearded laady and the pig with vive ligs, and on the roundabouts and the swing boats and the stame-'osses, and paid vor her to have a shy to the cokernits and a squirt of holy-calone on her hankcher. Kate was havin' the time of her life. Any fule cude zee that. Ginger cude zee it, and he wad'n gettin' a look in corner-ways.

He zeemed to railise that things was comin' to a pass, purty zoon. He veeled in his bones that if he did'n do zummat that very day, 'twude be too laate.

'And 'twill have to be zummat desprit, too,' he said to hiszelf.

So off he goes to think. He went into the rayfreshment booth to get zummin to think on. He thought on a quart o' beer.

Whether 'twas the quart or no I can't zay, but all-to-wance Ginger got a idaya in his mind. Not bein' accustomed to havin' idayas in his mind, it made 'n come over all giddy-like fer a bit.

But soon's the dizzyness had passed away he sot out fer the booth where Abdul the Prophet was carr'ing on with his fortune-tellin'. Ginger knawed that when Kate arrived at that one her wude want to have her fortune told, and Bert wude pay the money vor her to go in. So he determined to prepare the ground a bit.

Mrs. Prophet was outzide the booth, tryin' to intice the volks to pay their money to go in. But zome'ow business did'n zeem to be very rapid jis' then. Ginger went up to the door, and when Mrs. Prophet axed vor his money he said he wanted to zee the boss.

'You mus' pay yer zixpence fust,' her says.

'That's all right, missis. You let me go in and zee the boss. 'Twill mean more than zixpence to he.'

Her wad'n fer lettin' him go past, but Mr. Abdul had yeard what he said, so he poked a part of his nawse out droo the curtin and told Ginger to go inzide.

'Trade's a bit slow 's-mornin', id'n it?' says Ginger, when they'd both sot down.

'Dreadful slow,' says the Prophet. 'I dunnaw what's the matter with the volks. They daun' zim to care whether they gets a fortune or no. I ab'm took the price of a drink yet.'

Ginger tooked out two half-a-crowns from his pocket. He putt wan on the taable and showed Abdul t'other.

'There's the price o' sevver'l drinks,' he says, 'and I'll putt down the second wan if you do's what I wants.'

'What is it you wants?' says the Prophet, pickin' up the half-a-crown in case Ginger shude alter his mind.

So then Ginger explained all the whole rigmarole. He told Abdul he was in love with Kate, and how everything wude be all right if it wad'n vor Bert Yatton. And then he putt forth his scheme.

'Her's sure to come in yer, bim-by,' he said. 'And when her do her'll believe everything you tells her, 'cus her's that way inclined with regards to superstition, and over-looking, and the evil eye, and pixies and all such-like. Now I wants vor you to set her mind agin Bert Yatton and turn her ambition towards me. Tell her her mus' beware of a dark man with black hair and a black mustosh who's hankerin' arter her. Say he's a very bad chara'ter, and if her gets married to 'en her'll have nort but misery and strife all the days of her life. Let her have a-plenty o' that, so's her won't never want to look at the feller agean. You know how to wrap it up better than I can tell 'ee. And then tell her there's a fair man thinkin' about her and he's everything that's gude and straight, and if her haves he her'll never have cause to regret it, and all that sort o' thing. Have a gude look at me and then you'll be able to discribe the chap so's her can't make no mistaake. You word it so's her'll take it all een, and I promish 'ee faithful you shall have the other half-a-crown, and p'r'aps a bit more 'pon top o' that.'

Mr. Abdul laafed, and winkid at Ginger.

'You'm a fly burd, you be,' he saith.

'I wad'n born yesterdy,' says Ginger, and the prophet said:

'You laive it to me. I'll putt it all right.'

Ginger went out as happy as a lark. He was so happy he cude'n resist havin' a bit of a joke with Mrs. Prophet, and that's where he made a big mistaake to.

'My dear days, missis,' he said, 'you *be* lookin' well, sure nuff. You'll be jis' right for the County Show. I'm darned if you waun't take fus' prize and champion. They'll never be able to accuse your ole man of starvin' you, that's a sure thing. Wance round you, twice round the 'ood-rick.'

Now, if there was wan thing narked Mrs. Abdul more 'n any other, 'twas vor anybody to tell about her bein' vat. Her cude'n stand that at no price. Ginger thought he'd said zummin very amusin', but her did'n think zo. Her went in to the Prophet as wild as a hawk.

'What did that ojis little blaggard want with you?'

Abdul told her all about Ginger's scheme.

'The nasty, desateful toad,' her says. 'Jis' the sort o' thing I shude expect from 'en. Don't you do nothin' o' the sort.'

'There's another half-a-crown comin' from 'en,' says the Prophet.

'Don't you believe it. That kind o' feller wude'n come back and pay no more half-a-crowns arter he'd got what he wanted. If you do his dirty work you'll have to wissle fer the money. I shude larn he a lesson if I was you, and if you don't I will. If you praich up that yarn to the maid I shall tell her the truth when her goes out, so I warn 'ee. If her comes een, you tell her zac'ly the oppozyte, and not let her go thinkin' twice about that sassy ozeburd.'

Missis was master in that firm, and Abdul had to do what her told 'n, Prophet or no Prophet.

Kate went in, right nuff. Ginger had discribed her zac'ly, so Abdul owned her in a minute. He tracked out all the marks on the palm of her hand, and then he said there was a fair man her mus' beware of. He gived her a discription of Ginger Bidder, so's her cude'n mistaake who he was alludin' to.

'He's volleyin' you about very close,' he saith, 'but you muzzen have nort to do wai' 'n, 'cus he's two-facid and not to be tristed.'

Then he tracked out a vew more marks and said:

'I can also zee a tall dark man, very ansum, and he's goin' to be very rich. He's thinkin' about you now, and he id'n very fur away. He'll bring you gude luck.'

Kate thought 'twas marvellous that he shude be able to discribe everybody like that, and it showed that what he said must be right. Her gived 'n extry zixpence, 'cus her was delighted with her fortune.

O' coorse, Ginger thought her was bein' told zummin very differ'nt but he did'n zay nothin' to her that day. He let her have the night to think over what the Prophet had said and the next aiv'min he went to her houze to putt the ques'ion, as the sayin' is. He reckoned he'd only have to zay the word and everything wude be settled. You can imagine how he was tooked aback when her told 'n her was gwain to marry Bert Yatton. If her'd said the King o' the Cannibal Islands he cude'n 'a-bin more amazed.

'You daun't mane what you zay, Kate. Bert Yatton's a dark man. If you marries a dark man you'll have nort but misery.'

''Tis no such thing. Matter o' fact, I had my fortune told yesterdy, and Abdul the Prophet told me if I married the dark man what was thinkin' about me I shude be 'appy ever after.'

'You've got it all wrong. He said the fair man was the wan you shude have and the dark man was no gude.'

'How do you know what he said? You wasn't there. If you want to know, Alfy Bidder, he warned me agin a undersized little fair man with ginger eyebrows and his teeth pokin' out like tombstones, and a long nawse like a hoss and his veet stickin' out at a quarter to three. He discribed you to the very tick, and said if I married such a man as that I shude have bad luck all the rest of me life. He zee'd all that in the palm of my hand, so nobody waun' make me believe 'tid'n true.'

Ginger zee'd he'd bin had. He rished out from the houze, flied 'ome arter his gun and then went seekin' fer Abdul the Prophet. He vowed he's shoot 'n, and 'pon me zaul, if he cude 'a-got a sight aw'n, I verily believe he wude 'a-done. The volks warned Abdul, and he disappeared from the plaace jist in time. Ginger volleyed him up for months, and used to go to all the fairs vor miles around. It got so bad that poor Abdul cude'n visit any plaace in the neighbour'ude but was forced to bide away to a long distance, 'feared o' what Ginger wude do to 'en.

Fer ten years nobody ever zee'd Abdul the Prophet anywhere around thase parts, and his name was almost fergot. Kate Maddaway married Bert Yatton, but Ginger Bidder remained a zingle bachelor.

And when ten years had gone passed Abdul reckoned 'twude be safe for 'en to go back. He considered 'twude all be fergot arter all that time, and he was lostin' a lot o' money droo not being able to attend the fairs. So when the volks went to Muddlecombe Revel, there was the booth of Abdul the Prophet wance more.

Ginger had gived up gwain to sitch plaaces, 'cus he'd become a very busy man and cude'n spare the time. But when zomebody told 'n that Abdul had come back to the fair, he dropped everything, and started rinnin'. He did'n stap rinnin' till he got to the vield. He did'n stap then. He took wan glimpse around to vind Abdul's booth and went vor it like a long-dog. Missis Prophet did'n zee 'en till 'twas too late. Her tried to stap 'n, but Ginger managed to shove her a-wan side.

'I want to zee the boss.' And in he goes.

Abdul yeard the racket, and when he looked up, there was his old enemy, puffin' and blawin' like a unshorn sheep on Midzummer day. Abdul cude'n get out the door, 'cus Ginger was in the way. He give wan scraime, then he went down on the vloor and disappeared under the bottom o' the tent, like a rabbut in a 'awl. Ginger went arter 'en.

'Come back, yer,' he 'olleyed.

But Abdul was coosin' across the vield like a vox with the hounds behind 'en. Ginger went arter 'en. Abdul lookid around, zee'd 'en comin', and putt another spurt into it. He went around the minagerie, back an' vore between the stalls, in under the swing-boats, right droo the rayfreshment booth and out the other door, rinnin' vor dear life and Ginger graj'ly ketchin' vore to 'en. At last the poor ole feller 'itched his voot in a rope and went haid-long, and he was so exhausted with rinnin' he cude'n get up agean. His breath was all gone, and he was forced to give in and beg fer mercy.

'Mercy be blawed,' says Ginger. 'Why did'n you stap when I holleyed. I owes you half-a-crown and I wants to pay 'ee.'

Abdul lookid to Ginger with his eyes like taysassers. He was too much tooked aback to spaik. Then Ginger took 'n by the coat-coller and rised 'n up on his veet.

'Come along o' me,' he says, and he dragged Abdul to a plaace where they cude view the volks.

'Look over there,' he says, 'bezide the cokernit shies. Do you zee that gurt, coose-lookin' vat piece with the zeb'n scraalin' chillern hanged on to her tail, and a face that wude turn the milk sour at a gunshot away. That was Kate Maddaway wance. And do you zee that poor miserable-lookin' specimen bezide her, that her's bully-raggin' as if he was the scum o' the earth? That's Bert Yatton. If it had'n bin feer you I shude 'a-bin in that poor feller's shoes to-day. I shude 'a-bin the husband and vather o' that lot. Yer's the half-a-crown I never paid 'ee. And yer's another 'pon tap o' that. And listen yer! If ever you'm hard-putt-to, so that you dunnaw where to go fer the price of a drink, you come to Alfy Bidder, or if you can't remember that, say "Ginger". I'll never zee you starve, darned if I will. Not after what you've done fer me.'

MRS. SNELL'S RIDE

Us was riding into market as usual in Tom Zalter's carrier's cart, and Tom keeped on turnin' round in his driver's sate and eyein' Mrs. Snell up and down, and then turnin' back and passin' stoobid remarks to his hosses. 'Tis a 'abbit he've got of sayin' things to Prince and Blozzum when he wants to tantalize anybody.

Sevver'l times he done this, and to-last her said to 'en:

'What do 'ee want to keep lookin' to me vor?'

'I can't tell 'ee hardly, missis, what it is,' says Tom, lookin' back around again, with his haid a bit to wan zide as if he was tryin' to get a better view. 'What's wrong with you 's-mornin'?'

'There's nothin' wrong wi' me, but I shude think there mus' be zummin wrong wi' you, yer gurt mump'aid. You keep yer eyes to yer front and look arter yer hosses. They travels slow enough, gudeness knows, when you'm attendin' to 'em, but if you bides there with yer back turned to 'em they'll be stoppin' to ait the grass by the zide o' the rawd in a minute.'

Tom went on lookin' at her vor a bit, with wan eye screwed up, like as if he had'n yeard a word her said. Then he turned back to his hosses.

'Giddup, Blozzum! Prince-ah! Pull-up, 'osses. And not go pickin' out all the bumpy places, you terrifyin' toads you. Can't you zee Mrs. Snell id'n riding very comferable?'

'Did ever anybody come across such a provokin' vagabone?' says missis to we. 'Never 'appy unless he's keepin' on with his ole crams.'

Presen'ly Tom turned around again and had another look.

'What is the matter with you 's-mornin', missis?'

"'Twill be what's the matter with you in a minute, you chicky mommit,' her says. 'I'll give 'ee a scat with my anbrella, I will, if you keep on lookin' to me zo.'

'Well, why daun't you zit up straight?'

'I *be* zittin' up straight, ban' I? Why daun't you zit around straight, more like it.'

'No, you ban't zittin' up straight. You'm loppin' all auver to one zide, like a bag o' meal in a weel-barra. You've been up to zummin you did'n ought to. I knaw. And I shall vind out what 'tis, too, bevore the day's out.'

'Aw, trust you vor that,' says Mrs. Snell. 'You'm a proper Nosey-Parker, you be, if ever there was wan. Well, I suppose I mid-so-well tell 'ee all about it. You'm sure to vind out, zome way or 'nother.'

'Boun' to, missis,' says Tom. ''Tis impossible vor you to hide it, although you've done yer best. I shude zay, by the look of 'ee, that you ban't very comferable on the near zide.'

''Tis true as gospel,' her says. 'To tell 'ee the truth, I be most mortle oncomferable.'

'I can zee it. You've bin riding a hoss.'

'No, I ab'm bin riding a hoss.'

'You've bin ridin' zummat, or tryin' to.'

'I've bin ridin' a bicycle, if you want to knaw.'

'Dal'd if I did'n think zo,' says Tom, jumpin' round on his sate, and laafin' fit to bust hiszell. 'Prince-ah! Come-up, Blozzum, my dear! Darn if I daun't get a bicycle for you next. I'll bet you'd be able to zit down the nex' day as well as Mrs. Snell can. Whatever made 'ee do such thing, missis, a wumman of your age and weight?'

'Why shude'n I ride a bicycle the same as the rest?'

'There's no raison at all why you shude'n ride one the same as the rest. But you've been ridin' it differ'nt, by the look of it.'

'Aw, well, I was only a beginner. I ab'm larned to get in the way aw't.'

'You mean you ab'm larned to keep out o' the way aw't,' says Tom. 'What made 'ee undertake to ride a bicycle?'

'Well, 'twas like this-yer,' her saith. 'I've got a niece livin' into Barnstable.'

'Soosie Cumes, you mean?'

'That's right. You knaw Soosie, o' coorse. Well, her come to zee me, the beginnin' part o' the wik, to bide fer a vew days. Rode all the way on her bicycle, her did. Lovely new bicycle her'd got, so us got tellin' what a convaynient thing 'twas, and nice fer anybody to get about on. Wan thing led to another, and I

61

hap'm to zay how much I wished I'd larned the way to ride, 'cus 'twude be very handy fer me to be able to jump on a bicycle and flip into Week village, or auver to Nackaburge, better than fussin' about puttin' the hoss in the trap, and a sight quicker than walkin'. So then the maid says, 'Why daun't 'ee larn to ride now, auntie. You cude try on my bicycle, and if me and uncle was to hole 'ee up fer a bit you'd very zoon get in the way aw't.'

'"Do 'ee think I ever shude?" I says.

'"Of coorse you wude," her says. "Why shude'n you, as well as anybody else. If you was to try fer half-a-nower you'd be able to ride so-well as the next."

'Well, I did'n zee no raison why I shude'n, if it come to that, and James, he was all in favour aw't, 'cus it wude save he the bother of puttin' the hoss in the trap zometimes when he was in the middle of his work. He said he'd buy me a bicycle, if I cude ride 'n, and he was willin' to hold me up while I got in the way aw't. So arter us had finished tay, us tooked Soosie's bicycle out in the rawd fer me to try.'

'Poor James,' says Tom.

'You might well say that,' says Mrs. Snell. 'And what about poor me?'

'And what about the poor bicycle?'

'I wude'n say us done the bicycle a tremenjis amount o' gude,' says missis, 'although I wad'n so partic'ler sorry about that. It sarved the maid right fer edgin' me on to ride the blessid thing.'

'Well, how did 'ee get on, then, missis?'

'Get on! I don't remember very much about gettin' on; I was too busy all the time gettin' off. I reckon I got off o' thikky bicycle in every possible manner sep the right one, and on every part o' me body barrin' me veet. 'Tis no gude fer anybody to tell me a bicycle ab'm got the sainse to think. That wan had, anyway. He knawed when I was on the back of 'en, and he wude'n rest till he'd got me off again.

'When I was stood on the ground bezide 'en, he'd bide there as quiet as a lamb. I cude putt me hand on 'en, or ring his bell, and he wude'n move. He'd let me push 'n along the rawd, and he'd go as gentle and suant as our ole mare. I cude do any mortle thing I liked with 'en, so-long as I did'n try to ride the begger. But the minute I 'tempt' to get on his back he'd get so-wicked as a badger.

'"Now, auntie," the maid wude zay, "get up and try again. All you've got to do is to guide 'n straight and push yer veet around."

'So then her'd hold 'n up one zide and James wude support 'n the other, and I'd clim' up in the zaddle. The instant he veeled me on his back he'd start his capers to try to shove me off again. Fust he'd try to lay down James's side, and James wude be pushin' and haivin', and the maid pullin' and scritchin', and me hangin' on to the pair of 'em. Then us wude get 'n up straight, and James wude olley, "Now, then, work yer veet." But bevore I cude think which end me veet was, the ole bicycle wude make up his mind to lay down Soosie's side. Of coorse, her had'n the strength to hold me up, so James had to hang on as if he was pullin' a cow out of a pit. Then he'd knock his shin-bone up agin the treadle, and say things which ordnery times wude never pass his lips.

'After a bit they'd get the contr'y toad upright again, the both of 'em puffin' and blawin' as if they'd rinned a mile, and then they'd try shovin' behind. But the treacherous varmint, soon's ever they let go the hannle, he'd turned his haid right around, putt his vore wheel where the hine wheel ought to be, kicked up his hine-quarters, and bevore you cude say 'knife' there was me and the maid and James and the bicycle strawed all auver the rawd, till you cude'n tell t'other from which.

'Then, o' coorse, James went vor me and said 'twas all my fau't for not ketchin' hold the hannle proper.

'"What did you want to let 'n turn around there vor?" he says.

'"I did'n want to let 'n turn round there, stoobid," I says. "I wanted vor 'en to go the way he was lookin'."

'"Why did'n 'ee hold the hannles then?"

'"What's the use o' talkin' like that? You might as well expec' me to hold the tail of a graisy pig. I tell 'ee what 'tis," I said. "He daun' like gwain that way. He prefers to go tother way, so us'll turn the sulky toad around and let 'n go the way he wants to.'

'So us done that, and I climmed up in the zaddle wance more.

'"Now, keep'n hold tight," James said to me, "and not let'n go lookin' all auver the shop. If you keep his haid straight in front, his tail will come along straight behind."

'"If I knawed where his eyes was," I said, "I'd putt blinkers auver 'em."

63

'However, us had another go to 'en; me shakin' like a leave, James rinning down into strames o' swattin', and the maid laafin' so much her cude'n do nothin'. But us got on a lot better this time. The ole bicycle knawed he was gwain homeward, and 'twas a li'l bit down'eel, and I'm bothered if us wad'n gwain along so-straight as a line.

'"Keep 'n to that," says James, between his puffs, "keep 'n to that."

'"You tell the bicycle," I said. "'Tis no use tellin' me."

'All-to-wance the maid shouted, "Not go so vast, auntie, us can't keep up with 'ee."

'"Tid'n me," I says, "'tis the bicycle. Pull him back. I can't stap the toad."

'"Putt on the brake," her says.

'"What was the gude o' tellin' me to putt on the brake. I'd got hold to they two hannles as if me life depended on it, and I wude'n shift wan vinger for all the money in the world. Bezides, I did'n know where to go vor the brake, ner nothin' else. The only brake I cude thing about was whether I was gwain to brake me neck or no.

'And then, all of a sudden, I zee'd why the ole bicycle had become so gude-tempered, pretending. Us had come to a steep nap to go down over. The bicycle give one jump and went off like a train. I yer'd Soosie make a funny noise like anybody givin' their last gapse, and then her let go. Her cude'n hang on no longer. The bicycle, being free on that zide, wommled over towards James when he wad'n ready vor it, and he got his two veet 'itched wan in the other while he was rinnin', and I'm jiggered if he did'n go flyin' across the rawd like a shot out from a gun. I glimpsed 'n out o' the corner o' me eye jist as he disappeared into the brimmles.

'So then, o' coorse, the ole bicycle was free to do what he like, and away he goes, down over the heel, fast as he cude lick. It was like a burd flyin'. The furder us goes the vaster us went.

'I zee'd a derectin' paust down the bottom o' the heel. But the bicycle had zee'd it fust. He made fer that derectin' paust like a bull at a gaate. There was the whole width o' the rawd for he to go past, but he'd made up his mind, derectin' paust or nothin'. I done everything I cude to make 'n go a differ'nt way. I holleyed, "Wo". But he wude'n Wo. I shouted, "Wugback", and "Come-

'eer". And wude he take any notice? Not he wude'n. His one ambition was to go scat into thik derectin' paust, and nothin' on earth wude'n change 'en.

'And scat into the derectin' paust he went; me and all. Where I went arter that I can't tell 'ee fer certin; nor what it was I sot down upon I dunnaw. But 'twas zummin doostid hard and the wrong way up, and I ab'm sot down, what you might say comferable ever since.

'And when I wants to go shoppin' I shall walk, zame as bevore; or James shall putt the hoss in the trap. I've finished bicycles, thank you!'

THE WEDDING

1. JAN GETS OUT OF THE WAY

I'm a lodger up at our houze, that's all I be. In fac', I dunnaw that I be even so much as that. A lodger *have* got his rights, and he've got to be took some notice of, but I'm jiggered if anybody takes any notice o' me. I might be the cat about the place, as regards to matterin'. They daun't make no more odds about me than if I was a timbern image. Not so much. If I was a timbern image they'd be forced to move out o' my way. But 'tis me that do's all the gettin' out o' the way. And a purty vine ole rumpus if I daun't get quick enough.

I shude never 'a-thought that a man cude become so little account in his awn houze. I dunnaw that I ever considered mezelf very influential there, best o' times, if you understand my meanin'. But I've alwis bin traited with rispec', and my needs and requirements have bin considered as much as most men, and a lot more than a gude many.

But now, bless yer 'eart, I'm nobody. I don't count. I'm a vigger o' nort. All they axes of me is to keep out o' the way.

I knows 'tis turrable anxious times vor 'em, and that accounts vor it. The whole plaace is topsy-turby; mother and my darter Jane is on the go day and night, schemin' and plannin', palarverin' hours at a time, and they'll seek advice from any stranger. But if I attemp's to say a word on the subjic' I gets shut up in a instant, and told I dunnaw nothing about it. Which is perfec'ly true, but neether don't half o' they that has so much to say. If they what knows all about it was the only wans to give their opinion there wude'n be half so much yappin' and argifyin' as there is.

When it gets unbearable I goes off to the Black 'Oss fer a nower or zo, and that suits everybody all the way round.

66

THE WEDDING

I suppause you'm wonderin' what all the fuss is about. I dersay you'm thinkin', 'Ole Jan Stewer have had his nawse putt out o' joint. Zummat have gone wrong at home with 'n.'

P'r'aps you imagines I've done zummat wrong and upzot the missis. Well, 'tid'n that thees time, although 'twude'n be the fus' time, not by a long lot. Nobody id'n in a bad temper; I'll tell 'ee that much. Mother and Jane is enjoyin' theirzel's proper, although you'd think they'd got all the trouble in the world on their minds.

And I knaws what zome o' the men-volk will zay about the matter. They'll zay, 'Aw, 'tis the ole spring-clainin' gwain on, and the womenvolk be up to their eyes in it, and there's no plaace fer Jan to zit down to, ner a dacent meal, ner a bit o' paice, so he goes up to the Black 'Oss to excape out o' the way aw't.'

You'm wrong again. In zome ways 'tis zummin like the spring-clainin', only wiss if anything. With the spring-clainin' you knaws purty well what to expec', 'cus you've bin droo it bevore. So you knaws what to be up to. You've only got to take care not to rin scat into zummat which wad'n there a minute ago, or vall auver a bucket o' watter, or putt yer hand up agin the wall, or sit down on a cheer without lookin' to zee what's there, and you'll be all right. And, of coorse, you muzzen go axin' stoobid questions, like where your other butes is to, or what time you'm gwain to have yer tay. Things like that is ap' to erritate a wumman when her's doin' her best to balance dree cheers on a bookshelf with wan hand and roll back the carpet with t'other.

But this-yer caper is differ'nt, becus it have never hapm'd in our houze bevore, and 'twill never hap'm again, us only havin' the wan darter. And 'twill be in the eyes of the whole parish, and mother wude zooner die than aught shude go wrong. Her knaws that ole Sarah Tolley and Judy Western and wan or two more wude be only too plaised if they cude only vind zummat to critickise, and her's determined it shan't be zo if her can avoid it.

So now I expec' you've guessed what's the matter. Darter Jane is gwain to get married to the Young Jan. I calls 'n the Young Jan 'cus his name's John, same's mine. Zometimes us calls 'n Jan 'Enry to distinct 'n from me.

He comes up around most days, but I'm glad to zay he id'n took much more account of than what I be. If Nell Grinaway, the dressmaker, shude hap'm to be there when he goes in the rume, he'm 'sisted out again, quick, like a strange cat. Of coorse, Jane is very plaised to zee 'en and all that, but her've got other things on her mind, and he've got to zit about by hiszelf, or rade a buke, or come and talk to me. As fer mother, her'll go vor 'en like a pick-pocket, and tell 'n not to come there wastin' the maid's time. And Jane, her'll only laaf, and not stick up vor 'en, same's her wude any other time. And Jan 'Enry laafs too, 'cus he knaws he'm only in the way, same as me.

But when he comes to go home, nights, then the maid goes out to zee 'en as fur as the gaate, and I shude have thought they cude zay, 'Gudenight', in half the time if they was to try. But I derzay they don't try.

It have been all fixed up fer Jane and the Young Jan to get married the end o' this month, and 'tis the gettin' things ready and makin' all the ole fal-de-dals fer the maid to wear that have turned the whole place up-an'-down and in-an'-out. My dear days, what a fuss and scummer 'tis, to tettivate a maid up proper for a weddin'. Anybody wude think her was gwain up to Lunnon to be crowned Quane of England.

Well, there, it only comes wance in her lifetime, and I spause 'tis natteral her shude be excited about it. But I'm blawed if I knaws which is wist, hardly, her or her mother.

Of coorse, it have been a understood thing vor ever so long so I knawed it must come sooner or later. And about a wik or vortnit agone, Young Jan come to me and said he'd got everything in readiness and wude I give consent for fixin' the day.

But when it comes to sayin' you'll part with wan o' yer awn, 'tid'n aisy. Speshly when 'tis the only wan you've got, and such a wan as Jane. Zeems hard, when you've had her all these years grawin' up, and her's come to be a comfert to 'ee, and knaws your ways, and a pleasure to have about the houze, and then to go away and leave 'ee. And 'tid'n to say only gwain away vor holiday. When they goes away vor holiday you knaws that the space between 'ee is all the time gettin' smaller and smaller, and bim-bye they'll be back again. But wance they gets married the space is all the time gettin' bigger and bigger, and they never comes back. Not properly. I vancy 'tis turrable to think yer awn cheel will come to pay 'ee a visit and be all the time thinkin' about gwain home again. I dersay it waun' be quarter so bad when it acsh'ly comes, but that's the way it zeems to me now.

68

And zomehow or 'nother, I cude'n bring mezelf to zay the word, but I told the young feller he mus' spaik to her mother about it. 'Her've had most o' the bringing up o' the maid,' I said, 'and her's the wan shude zay when her shall go.'

Us was out in garden at the time, so he went in-houze to putt the matter to mother. And her went vor 'en, as I knawed her wude.

My Ann have got her veelings, same's any other wumman, and more than a gude many. But her hides 'em up in a differ'nt sort o' vashin' to what zome people do. Her can't a-bear vor anybody to think that her's soft-'arted, so her pretends to be angered whenever her's touched.

'What makes 'ee come to me?' her said. 'You've axed the maid, I spause, and that's all you cares about. What odds is it what I zay, after you've settled the whole matter?'

'I shude'n like to do aught without you was agreeable, mother,' he says.

'Rummage, agreeable,' says mother, lettin' into her old iron as if her was gwain to push 'n droo the taable. 'Fat lot you troubles about that. 'Tis all cut and dried, and you don't matter it one bit whether I be agreeable or disagreeable. But if I was Jane I'd send 'ee about yer business, double quick. If her took my advice her wude'n marry the best man in the world.'

'I don't want her to,' says Jan 'Enry. 'I wants her to have me. But if her did have the best man in the world he wude'n be gude nuff vor her.'

'Grammar! Gude nuff! You wait till you've had her vor a bit; you'll zoon vind out her id'n all that you thinks.'

'If her turns out as gude as her mother I shall be satisfied,' he says.

The crafty young begger. I vancy he knows a sight too much fer a feller his age.

'Don't you make no mistaake,' says Ann. 'Jane won't putt up with what I've putt up with.'

'Her won't be axed to,' he says, and then he winkid to me as gude as to zay, 'That's wan fer you, ole man.'

'Giddout, you'm all alike,' says mother. 'Bevore you'm married you'm gwain to do this, that and tother, and you promish all manner o' things, but after you've bin married a twul'-month you gets a very bad memory, and fergets half the wonderful things

you was gwain to do. And tid'n very much longer bevore you
fergets the other half. When you'm coortin' you'm vexed 'cus
you can't do enough; but after you'm married you'm feared of
your life you'm gwain to do too much.'

'Aw, well,' he says, 'if you'm so sot agin it, I mus' wait a bit
longer, that's all.'

I'm beggered if he have'n got a old haid on young shoulders.
He can twist and turn mother about a lot better than what I can.

'I wonder you've got the chick to tell about waitin' any longer,'
her saith. 'I shude think you've kep' the maid dallyin' about long
enough. Her cude have had a dizzen chances in the time. And
better wans, too.'

That was all he wanted, to get her to zay zummin like that. Her
cude'n go back from it, so the only thing was to hit upon the right
day. Mother reckoned it ought to be of a Wainsdy. 'You know
the old sayin',' her says:

> 'Mondy vor wealth,
> Chusedy vor health,
> Wainsdy the best day of all,
> Thursdy vor crosses,
> Vridy vor losses,
> Zatterdy no day at all.'

Jan 'Enry had got it into his haid he'd like it of a Mondy. I said,
'You'm after the wealth, I zee.'

'I shall get that in any case,' he says. 'Whichever day it is I shall
be the richest man in the world.'

'Now, don't 'ee start the ole rummage,' says Ann. 'You save
that up till you've bin married ten years. Her'll be able to
appreciate it more, tho. What made 'ee think of Mondy?'

''Tis the start of the wik,' he says. 'It zeems more vitty to me
than beginnin' in the middle. Bezides, Mondy id'n so long to wait
as Wainsdy.'

'Giddout, you gawk,' her says. 'You cude choose the Wainsdy
bevore, cude'n 'ee?'

'Then I shude want the Mondy bevore that,' he says.

'I shude think Jane's the right wan to name the day,' I said. So
Jane said her liked the Mondy, too, 'cus it zimmed the proper
day to start a new life, as you might term it.

'Did'n I zay 'twas all cut and dry?' says mother. 'They've got it all fixed up, bless yer zaul, and then they pretends to come and ax our views on the matter. Tell us the day o' the month while you'm about it, and finish with it.'

'Us thought June was a very gude month,' says Jan 'Enry, 'and us considered the twenty-vith wude do as well as any, if it was agreeable to you.'

'That's barely a month,' says mother. ''Twill be a turrable rish, but I dunnaw but what that's all-so-well. 'Tis fortunate Nell Grinnaway's home-about. Her's handy with the niddle. Us'll get her to come up by the day, and do what stitchin' there is to be done. You'll have to have zome sort o' cloas, I suppose. 'Twill mean a lot o' work, and thinkin' out. If you'm gwain to do it at all you mid-so-well do it proper while you'm about it.'

That night, me and mother sot on a bit after the maid had gone to bade. 'Tis a seldom thing us do bide up laate, but 'twas a coldish night and there was a nice bit o' vire on the hearth, and I suppose us was lofe to go away and laive it. So us sot there lookin' at it.

But us had'n got very much to zay. Matter o' fac', neether-wan of us did'n utter a word; only bide there watchin' the sticks burnin' and seein' shapes in the vire. At last I veeled I must zay zummat, so I said:

"Twill zeem turrable quiet yer when the maid have gone away.'

Mother did'n answer nothin'. Her only went on starin' into the vire.

Then her done what her daun' do very often. Her putt down her haid and had a gude cry.

2.   THE TROUSSEAU

What hullaballoo they makes about a weddin' now-a-days. I don't vancy it used to be zo when I was young. I can tell 'ee one thing. When I got married I tried to keep it as quiet as ever possible. The Zindy mornin' when us was gwain to be called to-church vor the fus' time of axin', I trapesed right over to Barleycombe, and there I bide till the last thing o' night. And then I come pokin' back arter dark, across the path-vields, like the dog

71

that stailed the mutton; feared of me life that zomebody wude zee me and start passing remarks.

And when the day come vor me to go to church vor the aschal sarrymony, I veeled more like creepin down a rabbut's 'ole. I was glad as a burd when that little caper was all over and I was able to get away out of it.

But, mind, I don't zay 'twas the zame with my Ann. Her did'n matter how much notice was took of her. The more the better. 'Twude have bin a turrable disappointment to she if half the parish had'n bin there to zee. Women-volk is differ'nt to men-volk in that rispect. If a man thinks anybody is gappin' at 'n he gets uncomferable drec'ly, and imagines there mus' be zummat wrong with 'n. But a wumman is never so happy as when everybody have got their eyes gazin' on her.

A body can understand it. When a wumman's gettin' married her tettivates herzelf up in all manner o' fal-de-dals and makes herzelf as han'sum as ever her can, and it wude'n be worth-a-while gwain to all that trouble if nobody was gwain to look. 'Tis what her've been lookin' vorward to all her life; and only right that her shude, 'cus arter all, to be a gude wive and a gude mother is the best thing a wumman can live up to. Not but what a man looks vorward to it. But 'tis differ'nt with he. He knaws that do whatever he will, he can't make hiszelf look purty, so he id'n so much enamoured of appearin' bevore all the volks.

Of coorse, you can't have a weddin' without a man, but to tell the honest truth, he do spoil the look aw't, and he'm only a nuisance.

The Young Jan vound that out, when it began to dray up nearer to the time. Us had many a laaf about it. He started comin' to me a lot more than ever he did bevore. Well there! There was no other place for 'en to go to. He wad'n wanted in doors where the dressmakin' business was gwain on. If he putt his nawse around the door they'd shoo 'en out, quick. Sometimes he'd go right in, in the middle o' the sewin', jus' fer devilment, and then there'd be a vine ole rumpus, and the things would be all pushed up in a heap so's he shude'n zee what they was.

He said to me wance, 'Strikes me dad, I ban't neether ornament ner use in this consarn.'

I said, 'You can take it from me, my zon, that you won't count vor very much, not vor the nex' wik or zo. Your turn will come later on,

72

no doubt, but jis' vor the present you've got to take a back sate. A man is the zame to a weddin' as the rattle is to a dunkey-cart; it can't go without him, but he don't add nothin' to the look of the thing. There's no call to bother about you. Everybody knows how you'm gwain to look, or if they don't know they don't care. But there's one comfort vor 'ee. If you shude hap'm to look a trifle more foolish than usual it won't matter very much, 'cus nobody won't be lookin' at 'ee. But if the maid's dress shude hang a half-inch too much to one zide, or ruck up under the arm-pits, or zome vine thing or 'nother, that wude be dreadful calamity, and ruin the whole affair.'

'I shude'n think Jane wude be one like that,' says the boye.

'What do 'ee mean, not like that?' I said. 'What did you want her to be like? A wumman's a wumman, and Jane id'n no differ'nt to the rest, and I shude'n wish vor her to be. Every wumman likes to be lookin' nice, more pa'ticly when her's bein' married, and if her shude hap'm to make the rest aw'm veel a bit jellis, her id'n gwain to cry her eyes out about that.'

I told him straight what I thought about it.

'Look yer, young feller-me-lad,' I said. 'I'll tell you wan thing, and you can believe it or misbelieve it, but if it wad'n fer the other women lookin' on, half of 'em wude never get married at all, 'cus they knaws they'm a sight better off single. But they'm feared if they daun' get married all the other women will say 'tis becus they never had the chance. Otherwise why shude any wumman want the fuss and bother of lookin' arter you or me all the days of their life? 'Tis a lucky job the women likes to show off in front of wan-tother. If it wad'n for that, hundreds and thousands o' men who've got gude homes to-day wude be cookin' their own grub and waishin' their own shurts.

'And Janes' the zame as the rest, bless yer 'art. If her wad'n, I shude have been for lettin' her zee the docter long ago. Her wude'n like to think her weddin' wad'n gwain to be the aiqual to Betty Row's or Julia Brinnacombe's or any other maid that her've zee'd married. 'Twill be only once in her lifetime, plaise God, so don't you go botherin' your haid if Jane gives her mind a bit more to her fal-de-dals for the nex' vew days than what her do to you. You'll get all the attention you wants arter you'm married, and a bit more zometimes, I daresay. If you don't you'll be more luckier than most chaps.'

The young feller laafed and tooked it the right way. I knowed he wude, 'cus he've got his haid screwed on proper.

But all the zame fer that, 'twas a middlin' gude caper with thikky-there ole trooso consarn. That's what the women-volk called it, 'trooso'. What it means egzacly, or where they got the name to, I can't tell 'ee. I think they must have read it in a cookery book. 'Tis what the gen'lvolks terms it, by all accounts, zo o' coorse, us mus' do the zame. Nell Grinnaway, the dressmaker, cude'n zay ten words without 'trooso' was wan of 'em, and I shude think, in her opinion, if you did'n have wan you cude'n be properly married. So I dunnaw how me and mother got on, 'cus I'm purty certin I never had such a thing, and I don't believe my Ann did eether. If her did, I never yeard of it. Be that as it may, Jane picked up the term someplace, and then mother larned it, and 'twas nort else but 'trooso' ever after.

They went from Dan to Beer-sheba lookin' vor a trooso. They had no less than vower journeys all the way up to Exeter to try to get one, and I dunnaw how many times into Barleycombe. I suppose they don't keep such thing in the village shop, and that accounts vor me never havin' zeen one. What it consists of I can't tell 'ee egzacly, and from what I can make out I ban't supposed to know, 'cus if I axed very many ques'ions I was told to shut up. I used to turrify the maid a bit zometimes and make wise I was gwain to guess. But bevore I'd guessed very many things her'd flip out o' the rume or else drow a book to my haid. But her and her mother cude'n spaik about nothin' else. I had foundations vor brexis, gussets vor dinner and 'corjean pleats vor tay. Zupper time I'd have a veed of shifton, creepy-sheen, nun's failings, scollops and fish-'ooks and a vew things like that. They'd rin their eye all over the world vor their ole trooso. Japanese silk, Maltese lace, Scotch tweed, Irish linen——

'Why don't 'ee have American cloth?' I said. ''Twude wear a lot longer.'

But I did'n get no thanks, even when I give 'em gude advice.

And what redeclus colours they did tell about, to be sure. Tomato rid, barley-straw yaller, apple-blozzum pink, corn-flower blue, crush strawberry. 'What about flat-pole green, or mash tettie white?' I said. But nothin' doin'.

Wan time they got their colours mixed up, and went telling about sacks blue and nigger brown.

74

'You've got that all wrong,' I said. 'Sacks is brown and niggers is black as my hat.'

But as I zay, they wude'n take no notice o' me. Just as well, per'aps.

Well, and then there was the matter o' bridesmaids. That was a purty vine scummer. They made out a list as long as yer arm, and then 'twas question which they shude strike out.

I said to the Young Jan, 'You'd better keep your eye on this,' I says, "cus you'll be expected to give all they bridesmaids a present a-piece and if 'tis half the quantity they've got on thikky list, I'm beggered if it won't cost you a small fortune.'

However, they cut it down to zix to-last, and that means that Jane will need to be extry careful, 'cus zome o' they what has been left out will be eyein' her up and down with the hopes they'll vind zummat wrong with the trooso. They'll spot it quick enough if her ab'm got it zac'ly right.

And then came the ques'ion about the reception, and that was a buster. Reception, if you plaise. 'Twas a maze-crack idaya whichever way you looked at it. But becus they had a reception down to Vive Ellums when Stephen Row's darter Betty was married, us must do likewise. What a barney that was, who shude come to the reception and who shude'n.

'Whatever do 'ee want that stoobid ole caper for?' I said. 'Reception be blawed. You dragged me down to the one to Vive Ellums, and I wude'n go the length o' me nawse to another such. I'd zooner walk ten mile tother way. Paasel of ole trumpery, I call that was. Shovin' and squaisin' into they rooms like a flock o' sheep in pens, stappin' on wan-tother's toes, tryin' to get a glass o' wine up to yer mouthe bevore zomebody knacked yer elbaw and slattered the lot and shakin' hands with volks you wude'n shake hands with if you met 'em in the strate vorty times.'

Then mother and Jane thought 'twude be a vine table-talk if they did'n keep up-zides with the Rows.

'Us don't want Betty Tucker that is now, Betty Row that was, drowin' it up in Jane's teeth that they had a reception and us did'n. Her putts on airs nuff as 'tis gudeness knows. Us don't want to pervide her with no more, if us can help aw't.'

And 'pon-tap o' that lot there come the weddin' caake, and that caused another kick-up. That wan had to be got from Exeter, zeem-zo. They called to the shop to zee about it while they was

75

seekin' vor a trooso. When they come back and told me what money 'twas gwain to cost, I was frightened.

'What wicked waste,' I said, 'drowin' away gude money on such ole trumpery. Two or dree o' Baker Webber's daugh-cakes wude veed the lot and not cost but a vew shullins. And nobody cude want nothin' better'n Baker Webber's daugh-cakes. They'm gude nuff vor me, and I'm certin sure they'm gude nuff vor anybody us'll be likely to have yer.'

Well, then Ann said I was'n to talk so fulish, and I said 'twas her that was talkin' fulish.

'How cude us have daugh-cake to a weddin'?' her says; and I said, 'Aisy, if us was to try.'

Well, and then you knows how 'tis in thase matters. When I started I did'n mean nothin' and I was only yappin' vor the sake o' yappin, as the sayin' is, more in joke than aught else. But wan thing laid to another, and like a gude many more fules, when I was contrydicted I beginned to take it sayrious. Instead o' laafin' and lettin' it go to that, as I shude 'a-done, I went argifyin', as if I was in airnest. And by Jo, after us had bin yappin' wan across tother vor a bit I beginned to think I railly *was* in airnest, and I volleyed it up, 'ammer and tongs, till us all lost our tempers.

That's the stoobid way trouble is caused, half the time. Of coorse, I cude'n leave it alone, and I started to rattle off about the expainse, and what money 'twas gwain to cost, and 'twas chuckin' it down the gutter, and all that old rigmarole. And once a body starts that sort o' rummage 'tis marvellous what things he will zay, and never stap to think how other volks is takin' it. Every time Ann put in her spauk I went wan better, and zo it got 'otter and 'otter, till to-last I tooked up my 'at and went out in garden. And I wad'n past the door hardly bevore I'd have give vive pound to take back what I'd said.

The maid volleyed me out, but I did'n yer her comin'. The fust I knawed she was there was when her took me by the arm.

'Daddy,' her says, 'I'm vexed you'm so upzot. 'Tis me that's in the wrong. I've been scheming out all these things and never thinkin' how the expainse was mountin' up. Us can leave out the reception, 'cus that *is* a waste o' money. And us can get a cake a lot cheaper than what us said. The people in the shop said they cude make a very gude wan vor half the money.'

76

THE WEDDING

Caw, darn my rigs, I cude have bit out my tongue by the roots. 'Us won't do no sitch thing,' I says. 'You don't think I meaned what I said, do 'ee, cheel? I was only jokin'. You won't laive out nothin'. Us'll have a reception that'll make Stephen Row's look like a mother's meetin' round the village pump. Us'll invite the whole parish, and then nobody won't be able to better it. You shall have what you deserves, my dear, the best that can be had, if I has to sell my long sleeve hat to pay vor it, what have been in the vamily ever since my gran'vather was married. As fer the cake, if you don't have wan a gude voot higher than Betty Row's I won't have the thing in the houze, so I warn 'ee. And you can tell your mother if her id'n dressed a lot smarter than Mrs. Row was I won't go to church with her. No, I'll tell her mezelf. And while us be about it, how many trooso's did Betty Row have? Only wan. Then darn 'ee, you shall have two.'

3.   IN PROPER STYLE

Everybody says the sarrymony went off fus' rate. I ab'm yeard a zingle body say a word to the cont'ry, from the highest to the lowest. And they was all there to the church, bless yer zaul, from the squire and his gude lady down to ole Stonecracker Jim, vor they was all partial to our Jane: rich and poor alike. I did'n ought to zay it about my awn cheel, I suppause, but if you went the length and breadth o' the parish I doubt if you'd yer wan word to her detriment. It alwis zim to come natteral to her to have a smile and a kind word, and if her cude'n zay a nice thing about a body her'd zooner keep quiet than zay a nasty wan.

I misses her most dreadful, 'cus her used to regard my veelin's jist as much as her wude any stranger; and you can't alwis say that about yer awn volks. I daun' mean to say that they trates 'ee bad, or aught like o' that. But you knows what 'tis when you'm together all day and every day. You'm ap' to get a bit crabbid zometimes and zay things which you wude'n zay to people who you only meets when you'm on your best behaviour. But zomehow or 'nother, Jane alwis zim to be able to look on the pleasant zide, and you had a job to bide in a bad temper, even if you wanted to. And zo I vinds it turrable hard to get accustomed to the plaace wihtout the maid about.

77

But you don't want to yer my troubles, fer certin, 'cus I expec' you've got nuff o' yer awn. You'm wan o' the lucky wans if you ab'm. I tries to look on the bright zide all I can and tells mezell 'tis all vor the best. The young has got to be considered fust, 'cus they've got their future bevore 'em. Us old volks muzzen stand in their way, 'cus us have got our future behind us, in a manner o' spaikin'. Our day is done and the night cometh when no man can work. 'Tis only by the old makin' way vor the young that the world keeps on keepin' on. You can zee that all around 'ee in nature, and 'tis the zame with human men and women as 'tis with the leaves on the bichen-trees.

Us all looks to have our day, and us can't have the day without the night volleyin' on behind. The zin can't alwis shine in one spot. He's on you vor a bit, and you veels the warmth. Then he travels on to shine on zome other body, and you finds that where you'm to 'tis gettin' dimpsey. Zome volks manages to keep theirzel's in the zin-shine a bit longer than what others do; and zome gets in the dimmets bevore their time, but us have all got to come to it in the end. 'Tis a gude thing to bide young as long as you can. Any fule can get old if he lives long nuff; but it takes a clever body, and a wise one, to keep theirzelf young.

But yer's me, praichin' up a sarment, instead o' tellin' about the weddin'.

Nobody can't deny but what us done the thing in proper stile. It cost me a purty penny, mind, but I was determined that the maid shude have the best that cude be got. Dree carriages I ordered from Barleycombe, with a pair of hosses to each, whereas the Rows made manage with two. And the weddin' cake was up to the heighth of my haid, where it stood on the table. As vor the reception—well there, that'll be the talk o' the plaace vor a gudish while to come. How ever all the volks squaised theirzells inzide the houze I can't think. I'm sure zome aw'm did'n get a proper breath from the time they got een till they got out agean. Speshly volks like Mrs. Snell, what wants a bit more rume than the average.

Ole Mother Grinnaway vowed and declared it tooked her ten minutes to get from the vore door-stap to the zideboard. Wad'n grum'ling, her wad'n. Her made a boast of it to show what crowds o' volks there was there.

I'm thankful to think it all passed off so well. 'Twas a sight better than what I anticipated. I tell 'ee straight, at one time I thought 'twas gwain to be a proper ole mix-muddle. Everything looked to me to be at zixes and zeb'ms. I cude'n zee vor the life o' me how us was gwain to get it all in order in the time. But 'twas marvellous how the women-volk managed to straight it all out at the last minute.

P'r'aps you've noticed that women is differ'nt to men in that rispect. If a man have got vorty things to do he mus' do 'em one at a time; but a wumman likes to start all vorty to-once. Likewise, when a man gets things in a muddle he's done. But a wumman starts with a muddle and graj'ly comes out straight.

The night bevore the sarrymony I considered us wude require another wik at the laist to get everything putt to rights. The quantity of jobs that was gwain to be zee'd to in the mornin' was amazing.

'You'll never get half aw'm done,' I said.

'Us will if you keep out of the way and not come turrifying anybody zo,' says my Ann.

'You waun't,' I said. ''Tis never possible.'

But they did. Somehow or 'nother they got everything attended to, although the very last minute bevore us started vor the church I yeard mother zay to Nell Grinnaway:

'Let me have a vine niddle, my dear, and a bit o' pink zilk dread.'

What her required that vor, or what wanted doing I can't tell 'ee, but I spause it got done all right. Anyway, the very next instant they stapped out the door to get in the carriage, and anybody to look at 'em wude think they'd bin sot twiddlin' their thumbs vor a nower; waitin' vor time to start, instead of rishin' about ever since day's-light, without hardly a minute to braithe. As vor me, I was rinning down into straimes o' sw'attin', and I had'n done nort 'seps keep gettin' out of other volks's way. But that meant a bit o' dappin' about, begad, 'cus there was dree o' they women each dashin' two ways to-once, and 'twas a wonder if one or other aw'm did'n want to be jist exac'ly where I was to.

Mother and the maid went out as proud as paycocks. How they cude face all they people like it I can't think. I'm blest if I knawed which way to look hardly. I never veeled more uncomferable in my life, 'cus they'd trigged me out like a merry-ander. They made me wear a long tail coat, and me long-sleeve 'at which I ab'm wore more 'n about dree times in the las' thirty years, a gurt ole hard coller that come purt' near up to me eyes, and a pair o' kid gloves. Purty vine lookin' objic' I was, I can tell 'ee.

'Stick me out in middle o' the vield,' I said, 'and you'll never get trouble with birds.'

'Daun' be zo vulish,' says Ann. 'You looks very well, considerin'. Any stranger wude'n knaw but what you was a proper gen'lman.'

'I mus' look a lot differ'nt to what I veels then,' I said.

To vinish matters, her sticked a gurt white vlower in me button-'awl.

'Putt zome blue ribbin round me 'at, and make a job aw't while you'm about it,' I said.

'Hold thee noise,' her said, 'and walk up straight; not go slouchin' and slammickin' along as if you'd done zummin you did'n ought to.'

'I have,' I said. 'I've come out too zoon for the Vith o' November.'

Mother looked a proper duchess, I'm blawed if her did'n. And as vor the maid, although I says it mezell, her was a credic to anybody. Purty as paint her looked in her white gown and all that flimsy trade over her haid and draggin' along behind. Gude job her did, too, 'cus everybody was natcherly kainin' to get a view of her and zo they did'n think about lookin' to me.

The Young Jan was there waitin' to the church. He'd made the best of hiszell, too. 'Pon me zaul, if he'd bin the zon of Lord Tomnoddy he cude'n have looked no smarter than what he did.

And they bridesmaids was a proper picsher. You'd go a long way bevore you'd vind half-a-dizzen such purty-lookin' maids again. Matter o' fact, I was zo busy lookin' to the bridesmaids that mother had to give me a jit on the arm to mind what I had to do.

So Jane tooked me by the arm and us went up droo the church. And although I cude'n zee mother I knowed her was lookin' around to all the people as gude as to zay, 'This is a eye-opener vor 'ee, I'll bet a guinea.'

I must admit, I never zee'd it done better in this parish, not by ordinery volk like we. 'Twas a better turn-out than the Rows, and I was very plaised vor the zake o' the women-volk.

Everything went off very nice. When paasen axed the Young Jan if he wude have the maid for his wedded wive, you cude yer 'n answer all auver the church. 'I WILL,' he said, as much as to zay, 'And I'd like to zee who cude stap me.' And when it come to the maid's turn, her spoke up brave, too. They said you cude yer her right back to the door.

Of coorse, I must be the one to go and do zummat fulish. Mother said her knowed I wude, 'cus I alwis do. 'Twad'n nothin' very much, but when the paasen said, 'Who giveth away this wumman?' that was my job. I shude have stapped vore and handed over the maid. But I was so aiger that the young volks shude do everything right, and spaik up proper, that I missed me turn and fergot what I had to do. So the bes' man give me a pug in the back, and that made me jump, so I ups and says, 'I will,' tap o' me voice. I wad'n s'posed to spaik, railly, so he give me another jit, and that putt me into a proper flummox, and I stood there like a molten image. However, the maid jis' lookid up to me with a bit of a smile and putt her hand in mine, so that brought me back to me sainses and I done me juty.

My Ann wanted to take me to tackle vor it arterwards, and make out I spoiled it, 'cus I wad'n ready to the very tick. But I got out of it all right.

'Git-out,' I says. 'I wad'n gwain to let the people think I was as aiger as all that to give away the maid. I wanted to hang on to her so-long as ever I cude.

When the sarrymony was all over and the papers all signed, us made up a precession and trapesed back droo the church. But this time my maid was lained on another man's arm, and not on mine, and that's when I properly beginned to railise that her wad'n my maid no more. Her was gone. As I watched 'em marchin' off down the aisle I veeled as if all the joyful part was finished so-fur as I was consarned. 'Twas like zomebody hungerd, lookin' droo a winder at other volks feastin' and drinkin'. I zee'd that mother was gettin' full about the eyes, too, and veelin' all about vor her pocket-ankcher. But her wad'n used to her new clothes and did'n know where to go vor wan. Zo I passed her over my clane ankcher, and her tooked it like a lamb. Her was glad to lain 'pon my arm too, poor zaul, gwain down droo the church.

But when us got to the door, there wad'n no more time to think about bein' mooty-arted, or down-couraged. The volks had all flipped out, and 'twas much as anybody cude do to make

81

haidway. They'd all brought this-yer ole confetty trade, and you cude scarcely zee vor it. And they did'n use it all on the young volks, neether. They must 'a-drowed cart-loads to me and mother. I had a moutheful, and it went all down inzide me coller, and everyplace.

There's wan thing about the old confetty, 'tis a bit saufter than rice, but hawful stuff to get rids of. 'Twas amazin' the funny places us vound bits about, vor wiks arterwards.

Everybody in the parish must have went to the reception. But there was enough and to spare. Trust mother to zee to that. And what if they was squashed up a bit? Nobody did'n matter it. The more they was squaised the more they laafed.

In the midst of all the noise and chitterin' Ned Annaferd stood up-tap of a cheer. Several shouted out, 'Order.' And then I'm jiggered if Ned did'n make a spaich. 'Twas jis' like a rale spaich, too. If you had'n knawed, you wude'n tell the difference. How he do's it I can't think.

'Ladies and gen'lmen,' he saith. 'I be one of Jan Stewer's oldest vriends, and therefore I be gwain to taake it on mezell to prepose a toast, and one which I'm sure one and all will rispond to in a proper manner. Me and Jan was boyes together, went to skule together, got into mischief together and grawed up together. There's a gude many else in the rume have knowed Jan Stewer all their lives, and us be boun' to confess he's a sight better feller than anybody wude think to look at 'en. As fer Mrs. Stewer, us all knows her's one o' the very best. There id'n a zaul in the parish but what have got a good word to zay for the pair aw'm, and us hopes they'll live long and happy vor many years to come. But what I wants 'ee to do now, is to drink health, happiness and prosperity to the young couple. Zome of us have knowed Miss Jane (I beg your pardon, Mrs. Jane, I shude zay) ever since her thought her toes was made to be eat, and us all knows that her's as swit as her is purty-lookin'. I can tell Young Jan to his faace that us be all in love with his wive, and he can take it or laive it. If I'd bin thirty or vorty years younger he'd have had a lot harder job to get her than what he have. And he ab'm had a very aisy one as 'tis, 'cus there's a-plenty yer present in the rume now wude have bin only too glad to be the happy man in church to-day.'

Everybody laafed, and several o' the chaps said, 'Yer, yer,' and that made 'em laaf all the more.

THE WEDDING

'So the Young Jan must think hiszell a very lucky man.'

Jan 'Enry looked up and said, 'I be lucky, Mr. Annaferd.'

But Jane spoked up and said, 'And so be I lucky,' her said.

'Well,' says Ned, 'I ban't gwain to zay but what that might be zo. Us ban't acquainted with the Young Jan hardly so much as what us be with Jane. But what us have zee'd of 'n, the last year or two is all to his credic, and us knows he sarved his country well in the war, which he'll bear the marks to his dyin' day. Us believes he'm worthy o' the bride he'm takin' away, and that's sayin' a gurt lot. But I give 'n fair warnin', if he daun' trate our li'l Jane in a proper manner, it won't do vor 'en to show his nawse in this parish.'

Us all laafed again and drinked health to the bride and bridegroom, and everybody gived dree cheers with one or two extry drowed in vor luck, and then Jane and her man got into the moter and drived away. And thikky-there stoobid Lias Buzzacott fastened a old boot on behind.

LIAS IN TOWN

I dunnaw what *you* thinks about it, but I reckon I'm intitled to have a medal, or a sustificate, or zummin o' the sort for venturin' to take my wive and Lias Buzzacott to Lunnon, both at the zame time.

When you come to weight it all up, that was a middlin' big contrac' vor me to undertake. Noble, I calls it; or else fule-hardy, whichever you like.

In the fust place, I shude have trouble enough to vind me way about if I was all alone by mezell, with no other body to consider. I shude get bewildered every wip and turn. Then you come to take my Ann as well, who alwis considers that everything I propose must be wrong vor certin, and if I zay, "Tis down yer on the left,' will be convinced it mus' be up there on the right, even if her's never been near the place bevore. And then you add on top o' that lot that gurt gawk of a Lias Buzzacott, who never had'n been to Lunnon bevore in his life, and spent most of his time walkin' backerds with his mouthe wide open, gappin' about like a zix-year-ole cheel in a minagerie, and bumpin' into all the volks who thought he was gwain the oppozyte derection, and you'll zay I dezarved to get zummin beneficial.

Lias was the wist nuisance. Mother was bad nuff, gudeness knows, 'cus her'd stap to every turnin' and declare us ought to be gwain a differ'nt way to what us was, and her'd want me to go and inquire from every policeman her zee'd. But then, I did know where her was to, 'cus I cude yer her tongue gwain all the time like a mill-clapper. If I happend to lose sight of her in the crowd I'd only got to listen vor a minute.

But Lias had got to be watched like a puppy bein' took out vor the fus' time. He cude'n go vore a lan'yard without stappin' to gap at zummin. Drec'ly he zee'd aught a bit coorious, or a buildin' higher than the rest, or a dummy in shop winder, or anybody dressed a bit strange, he'd stand still and stare like a cow thinkin', and ferget all about we, or where he was gwain, or anything o' the sort.

All of a sudden us wude vind he was missin', and then 'twude be, 'Where fer gudeness gracious saake have the gurt fule got to now?' I'd look all around; not a sign of 'n. So I'd have to go back and seek vor 'en, and there he'd be gappin' to zome stoobid ole item or 'nother. And when I took 'n to tackle vor it, he'd zay, 'You'm missin' half aw't, Jan. There's a black man over there, lookee. You wude'n zee a black man to Muddlecombe once in a hunderd years.'

Once us lost the gurt mump-'aid altogether. Cude'n zee 'en no-plaace.

'Aw, let 'n lostee,' says my Ann. 'Zomebody will vind 'en bim-bye, and they'm welcome to 'en. I'm zick and tired o' lookin' arter the gurt looney.'

'Us can't do that,' I said. 'Us brought 'n yer and us mus' take 'n back, daid or alive.'

With the zame I yeard zomebody laaf above all the roar and racket. I knawed there was only one body in the world cude laaf like that, and that's how I vound the nuisance. He was stood lookin' to a chap with a lot of li'l images selling in the strate. When the chap putt wan o' they images down on the path he'd turn tap over tail and kick up his legs in the air. Every time he done that Lias wude roar laafin', and every time he laafed the volks wude all turn around to zee what all the noise was about.

'Come on you stoobid-haid,' I said. 'Why don't you think where you'm gwain, and not bide gappin' to every li'l fiddle-faddle.'

'Yer, Jan,' he 'olleyed out, as if he was in the middle of Ten-acres instead of Lunnon strate. 'You come and watch this-yer li'l mommet turn auver tap-an'tail. I'm beggered if 'tid'n zac'ly like life. Let 'n do it again, mister.'

'You'll zee scores like that,' I said, 'and if you'm gwain to bide lookin' to 'em all us'll never get no-plaace.'

'Shall I?' he says, as plaised as Punch. 'I'm blest if that wad'n worth comin' to Lunnon vor. Darn if I daun' have one o' they li'l toads and take back to Mrs. Snell; and one vor Mrs. Endycott. What be 'um, a penny a-piece?' he said to the chap.

'Don't you go chuckin' yer money about like that,' says the feller. 'They'm one shullin' each.'

Lias nearly had a vit. 'I ab'm got me cheque-book with me now,' he says, 'but nex' time you'm passin' droo Muddlecombe you call to my private residence, and I'll sell a bit o' property and buy a couple.'

'More likely you'll get what you'm axing vor,' the chap said, lookin' very nasty. I zee'd there was gwain to be a bit of a scummer, 'cus he wude'n frighten Lias if he was as big as a houze. So I ketch 'n hold by the arm and drag' 'n off. The mother had a vew remarks to make 'cus I'd left her all that time alone in the strate. Anybody might aisy have rinned off with her, zo her said.

'Not in the day-light they wude'n,' I said, and I thought her cude take it which way her liked. But 'twill give 'ee zome idaya o' the trate I had gettin' they two across Lunnon.

You wude 'a-died laafin' if you cude 'a-zee'd Lias when us arrived to thikky-there grand hotel, where us ordained to stay while us was in Lunnon. Some 'Palace', 'twas called, and a very gude name vor 't I shude think. I never wad'n inzide of a rale palace but I wude'n say there cude be all that differ'nce. O' coorse us cude 'a-went to a smaller plaace, but us was determined to do the thing proper, the vew days us *was* there, and 'twad'n so turrable much more costly when you come to weigh it all up.

When us got inzide the door Lias stood like a fule, frightened. 'Us have come in the wrong plaace, Jan,' he said. 'This mus' be zome vine gen'lman's mansion.'

'Then you can vancy you'm a vine gen'lman, Lias,' I said, 'and make yerzell at 'ome.'

'What do 'ee mean, "make mezell at 'ome?" Do you mean to zay I can walk about on they carpets where I like, and zit down in they aisy cheers?'

'Ees, and stan' on yer head if you mind to.'

Lias cude'n hardly take it een and he walked about like a man in a draime. There was no fear about losting him now. He volleyed us like a lamb.

'This id'n a houze, Jan,' he says, "tis a parish. I might as well wish 'ee "Gude-bye", 'cus if I loses sight of 'ee I shall never vind 'ee again, that's a certin sure thing.'

Us went over to the young laady behind the counter and inquired about the bed-rumes where us had to slape to. Her told Lias his rume was number zeb'm hunderd and vorty-wan. You shude 'a-zee's his face.

'What do that mean?'

'That's your rume vor to-night,' her says. 'You'll vind the number on the door.'

'Well, where is it vor gudeness saake?' says Lias. 'Up the other end o' the strate?'

Her laafed. 'No, upstairs.'

Lias cude'n vathom that. 'You daun' mean to zay there's over zeb'n hunderd rumes in this houze?'

'Ees, and over a thousand.'

'What, do 'em reach up to the sky?' he says. 'I shall never vind mine out o' that lot.'

'Ees, you will,' says Ann. 'Pick up yer kay, and us'll go up the lift.'

You zee, mother had bin there bevore and her was anxious to let Lias zee that her knawed the way about.

When us got inzide the lift there was sever'l there already, so when the chap shut the door there wad'n only rume to stand. Lias did'n think very much of it.

'No winder they can have a thousand rumes,' he says, 'if this is all the size they be.' And then he said to the lift feller, 'Is this number zeb'm hunderd and vorty-wan, 'cus if it is I don't think very much of it.'

Zome o' the volks turned their faces round to the wall to laaf, but bevore the chap cude answer, the lift started gwain up. Lias give one shout and ketched hold to a perfec' stranger. 'Look out,' he saith, 'the whole blimmin' place is vallin' down.'

This time the volks didn trouble about turnin' their haids around. They bust out laafin' where they stood.

'Hold thee baal, stoobid,' says Ann. 'This is only the lift to save 'ee from trapesin' all up the stairs.'

'My hyvers,' he says, ''tis come to something when you goes to bed by train.'

When us got out from the lift, us was in a plaace with long drangways gwain off in all derections. I said to Lias:

'You walk straight along there 'genst you comes to your number, and that'll be your rume. Open the door with thikky kay

87

and go right in, as if the plaace belonged to 'ee. When you've had a bit of a waish and made yerzell look vitty, come back along yer and knack to number zeb'm hunderd and eighty-vower. That's where us'll be to, and us'll all go down and have zome tay.'

'Sounds all right,' he says, 'but 'tis my belief once I leaves 'ee I shall never zee 'ee again. Bezides, I ab'm got me bag, and there's me brish and comb and everything else in that one.'

'You'll vind he in yer rume,' I said.

'You daun' zay zo,' says Lias. 'Well, he must have more sainse than what I've got. I shall never vind me way about yer. I said 'twas a parish, but 'tis a town, begad.'

'You can't mistake it,' I says, ''cus the numbers is all in alphabetical order.'

So I went and tettyvated mezell up a bit, and us waited and waited vor Lias but he did'n come, so to-last I said to mother, 'I'll flip along and zee what he's up to.'

I went along and knacked to Lias's door.

'Come een, whoever you be,' he says.

'I can't come een till you turns the hannle,' I says. 'You can't open thase-yer doors outzide without you've got the kay.' So Lias let me een.

'Why, you'm all in the dark, Lias. Why don't 'ee make a light?'

'Make a light,' he says. 'I've strick a boxful o' matches and I can't vind a bit o' cannle in the plaace.'

'Git-out, you gurt dunkey, you daun' want a cannle. Push up thik li'l braasen thing behind the door.'

Of coorse, soon's he done that the 'lectric ketched avire. He purt' near jumped out of his butes.

'My dear days,' he says, 'there's nothing like this to Mud-dlecombe.'

'Look sharp and waish, Lias. Us be wastin' time.'

'Can't waish, Jan. There id'n a joog o' watter yer. I've lookid all over the place vor wan.'

'What do 'ee want a joog vor, stoobid? Can't 'ee zee they taps pokin' out over the basin. Turn they on, you'll get all the watter you want.'

'I shall never larn it all, Jan. Down to Muddlecombe you'd have to go out to the pump to aiqual that.'

The nex' minute Lias was squailin' like a pig, and hoppin' all around the rume.

'What's the matter, now?' I said.

'Matter! My jaly, that watter's scal' 'ot.'

'Well, can't 'ee rade, mump-'aid? What do you think H-O-T stands vor, "ice"?'

'I shan't in future,' he says. 'But who ever wude expect 'ot watter to come out from a tap? You wude'n make 'ot watter come out from the pump if you was to try vor a year.'

'When you'm properly vitty,' I said, 'us'll go down and have a dish o' tay. I can do with it.'

'Can't us push a nob and make the tay come up droo the vloor?' he says. ''Twude'n surprise me in the laste, arter what I've bin droo.'

'Us'll go back and pick up the missis, and then vind the old lift again.'

So I laid the way along the landin'. I cude have sweared 'twas all straight road and I cude go right to the spot, but jiggered if I did'n get mixed up zome'ow. I kep' tryin' fresh turnin's when us cude'n go straight no furder, but I did'n zeem to get to my number. I did'n let on to Lias that I wad'n sure about the way, but I kep' watch on the numbers out o' the corner o' me eye, and I thought if I went on long enough I sure to come to it bim-bye. Presen'ly Lias said, 'You lives a long way off, Jan. I reckon they ought to have a tram yer, as well as a lift.'

'Tid'n much furder, now,' I said. 'Only jist along yer.'

I hoped to gudeness 'twas true. With the zame, Lias stopped.

'Wude 'ee like to rest a bit, Jan, bevore you tramp any furder? This is my rume, so I can invite 'ee in.'

I'm bothered if 'twad 'n, too. Us was back where we started to. Did'n that gurt gawk laaf! He had to lain up agin the wall to stan' upright. I thought he was gwain to bust a blid-vessel, and I hoped he wude.

'How does the chune go again, Jan? "Yer we go round the mulberry bewsh."'

'Daun' be so daaft,' I said. 'I wad'n thinkin' where I was gwain. I cude go there with me eyes shut.'

But beggered if I cude. I cude'n go there with 'em open. Darn my rigs if I did'n come back to the zame plaace again. And to-last I had to ax wan o' the maids which way to go.

'I'm as glad as a burd, Jan,' says Lias. 'I was wretched bevore, 'cus I thought I was the only dunkey in the party. But I veel happier now.'

When us got in the plaace where us had our tay to, Lias's faace was a picsher. His eyes was like tay-sassers, and the mouthe of 'n was like a rabbut 'ole.

'Call this a rume?' he says. 'Why, I've ploughed up vields smaller than this. And where for gudeness saake did all thase volks come from? If you was to send away as many as there is in the whole parish o' Muddlecombe you wude'n notice they'd gone. 'Tis never true. I shall wake up presen'ly.'

Us had to walk around zome time bevore us vound a spare taable, and the volks sot down had to look spry that Lias did'n stap on their veet. He was so busy gappin' about that he cude'n stop to look where he was gwain to. However, us found wan to-last.

'I've got a gude job vor you, Lias,' I said. 'Jis' ketch the eye o' wan o' they purty maidens with the white cap, and ax her to bring along the tay.'

That suited Lias down to the ground.

'Will her understand what I say, do 'ee think? I don't vancy they spaik the zame language up yer as what they do down-along.'

'I darezay her'll sense the drift aw't,' I said.

Lias did'n wait vor her to come along. He went arter her.

'Us wants tay ver dree, miss, plaise.'

'You want who?' her says.

'No, not "who?" "What?" Tay ver dree.'

'I don't know him,' says the maid.

'Yas, you do. Tid'n a him. Tay; deesh o'tay, to drink, ver dree; wan, two, dree. Tay ver dree.'

'Is it tea for three you want?'

'That's right, miss. That's what I said.'

So her took along our tay, and when her cude'n help smilin' to Lias he thought 'twas becus he was a gude-lookin' young feller. He lied back in his cheer and spraid out his veet.

'Well', he says, 'I've of'n wondered what it veeled like to be the Laurd Mayor, and now I knows.'

90

A PECK O' CIDER

I wude'n zay the conversation which went on in the days of the ole Carrier's Cart on the way to market was alwis aidifying. But what cude you expec'? When the zame half-dizzen of 'ee meets time arter time, you can't alwis hatch up sayrious matters to tell about. And there's occasions when you don't veel like talkin' sayrious. One body will start off with zummin fulish, and then 'tis which can make hiszell the most redeclus. And I dunnaw that it done very much hurt. A bit of a laaf and a joke zometimes is like graise to the wheels, and makes it aisier to jog along over the rough plaaces. I mind one day in pa'ticler when us was all in fulish mood, and I'll tell 'ee the conversation what went on. Us had had a lot o' rain, I remember, and when Mrs. Snell got in her said to Tom Zalter, the draiver:

'Nice weather in between the showers, Tom.'

'I can't zay, missis,' he says. 'I ab'm bin there.'

'You ab'm bin where?'

'In between the showers. There ab'm been no "in between" out our way. The nex' shower have started where the last one left off to.'

'Never mind, Tom. You must try to remember the zin is alwis shinin' zomewhere. A paasen tole me that once.'

'That's the zort o' thing a paasen *wude* tell 'ee; and a fat lot o' gude it is too. You might-so-well tell me there's sixty 'ogs-haids o' cider up to Farmer Wonnacott's. What comfert is that to me, with me tongue claivin' unto the roof o' me mouthe?'

'What gude wude zixty 'ogs-haids o' cider be to you, anyway? You wude'n know what to do wai't if you had it.'

'Aw, I dunnaw, missis. I dersay I cude make it last over the weeks-end, and p'r'aps I cude get zome more on the Mondy.'

Then Mrs. Endycott cheemed een.

91

'I'd be ashamed to talk like it, Tom Zalter. All you thinks about is drinkin' cider.'

"Tis untruth, Mrs. Endycott, and you've no right to zay sitch thing.'

'I'd like to know what else you thinks about, then.'

'Why, zometimes I thinks about drinkin' beer.'

"Tis pity you don't try to think about zummin better, then, that's all. Makin' yerzell lower than the animals. Why don't you take a lesson from yer own hosses, and drink watter?'

'Why don't you take a lesson from 'em and eat hay?'

'Say zummat to Tom Zalter for me and shut 'en up, Mr. Annaferd,' her says. 'He've got a back-answer for everything I says.'

'Tid'n very much gude you comin' to me, Mrs. Endycott,' says Ned Annaferd. 'I ab'm got much patience mezell with the volks what tries to make out 'tis wickednesss to drink a joog o' cider. I injoys a drap o' cider as much as anybody when I veels like it, and 'tis redeclus to zay 'tis wrong.'

'There's zome what don't stap when they've had one,' her says. 'They must have a dizzen, and then they'm proper mazed, and fit vor nort.'

'I knaw there is zome like that, missis. But you never knowed me take more than was gude vor me.'

'Very true, Mr. Annaferd. But if there wad'n none about nobody cude'n come to no harm with it.'

'Zame thing applies to watter,' says Lias Buzzacott. 'Poor ole Joe Wessmacott drowned hiszell twelve month agone come Lady Day. If there had'n bin no watter about he cude'n 'a-done that, cude 'er?'

'If Lias Buzzacott is gwain to start,' says Mrs. Endycott, "tis time vor sensible volk to lave off.'

'That's need'n stop you from keepin' on, missis,' says Lias. 'You might argue the zame way about scores o' things. There was Roger Tugwell hanged hiszelf to a beam with one o' Farmer Urferd's plough-lines. So you might-so-well zay all rope shude be done away with and then nobody cude'n hang theirzells.'

'If such thing was to come to pass,' says Tom Zalter, 'I shude advocate leaving enough vor Lias Buzzacott.'

'Bless yer zaul,' says Mrs. Endycott, 'his sort never hangs theirzells. They takes too much delight in making theirzells a nuisance in this world to go to the next.'

'Lias cude'n hang hiszell, anyway,' says Tom. 'He've got too hard a neck.'

'Well, you'm on with a nice topic, I mus' zay,' says Mrs. Snell, 'tellin' about hangin' and drownin' and all the rest aw't. If you can't vind nothin' better than that to tell about 'tis better you bide quiet, 'pon me word.'

'Us was tellin' about cider bevore Lias cheemed een,' says Tom, 'and I dunnaw what better subjic' you cude want than that.'

'There you goes again,' says Mrs. Endycott. 'Alwis got cider in your mind, you have.'

''Tis the only place I've got any this mornin', then,' he says. 'And the only place I'm likely to, zeems-zo. When ole Jan Grant use to ride in my cart he used to take along a firkin o' cider as rigler as clockwork. Never knowed 'en to miss. But times has altered. I never gets axed now if I've got a mouthe. All you lot wude zee a man starve. And got plenty home spoilin', I'll make a bet.'

'Never mind, Tom,' says Mrs. Snell, 'if you look up around my place to-morra you shall have a joog-vul.'

'I knows that, missis. But I shude get that anyway. 'Tis the li'l drop of extry, unexpected, that makes all the differ'nce.'

'How much cider do you reckon ole Jan Grant gets droo in the coorse of a day, Tom?' says Ned.

'Well, maister, I've yer'd the ole feller zay scores o' times, back-along, that he alwis considered his allowance was a peck a day.'

'Peck a day!' says Mrs. Endycott. 'Two gallon in a day? You don't mean to zay he drinked it.'

'What do you think he done with it, waished in it? Of coorse he drinked it, and that wad'n includin' what he termed the odds's. If he met with anybody accidental and lookid into the Black 'Oss, or if he called any place on a matter o' business and wet the bargin, that was over-plush, and did'n count. He alwis reckoned to drink a peck of his awn cider between dayslight and dark.'

''Tis owdacious,' says Mrs. Endycott. 'I don' zee where he cude putt it to.'

'Aw, bless yer 'art, ole Jan cude alwis vind a place to putt it to. He reckoned if he drinked a quart he'd sw'at out that lot in half-a-nower.'

'I derzay there was zome truth in that,' says Ned, ''cus I consider Jan Grant was hardest workin' man in this parish in his day, and I daun' care where you went vor the next.'

'That's a true word, maister, if you never says another,' says Tom. 'I've yeard my ole vather zay, that years agone, when they was mowin' or reapin' with the scy'e, bevore machines was invented, there wad'n a man anywhere in the distric' cude keep vore with Jan Grant. He'd alwis go in laider, and he'd offer to pay a shullin' to anybody what cude ketch his heels with their scy'e, arter the fus' dizzen swaths. But there was never a number two cude keep within reach of 'n. He'm failin' a bit latterly, although he'm worth two o' zome o' the youngsters, now. I zeed 'en only a wik agone las' Chewsdy, up to Dree Ellums, ploughin' thik steepy vield, back o' the chapel. Cock-eyed vield to plough, that is, if ever there was one. All shapes he is, like the last pancake, and up and down like the back of a camel. But I'm jiggered if ole Jan wad'n puttin' in zome butiful work; cuttin' in as straight as a line, and every vorr' as if he'd had a straight-edge to it. I said to the ole feller:

'"Jan," I said, "when do you ordain to wear out? I'm beggered if you ban't as gude as ever."

'"No, I ban't, Tom Zalter," he said. "I ban't the man I was."

'"What makes 'ee think that, maister?" I said.

'"I daun' think, I knaws it. Only yesterdy," he says, "when I'd drinked my zeb'mth quart, I did'n zeem to matter whether I had the 'ighth or no. Such thing never happened bevore. 'Tis the fus' signs of old age creepin' on, Tom Zalter."

'"Old age be blawed, Jan. You ban't a lot over zemp'ty, be 'ee?"

'"I be in my zemp'ty-'ighth, Tom, but zometimes I veels older. I reckon I shall go like my poor ole vather," he saith. "He had to jack up work when he wad'n but 'ighty-vive, and he did'n live but vower year arter that. And the fust signs of his gwain down-'eel, was lostin' the power to take his liquor proper, although he never wad'n what you wude call a drinkin' man. Vive quart a day was about his average, and when he dropped back to vower, and then to dree us knowed he wad'n gwain to last a lot longer. I was only about o' vifty when poor ole vather beginned to fail, but I minds it as if 'twad'n but yesterdy."'

'Pity he didn't start to go back a bit zooner,' says Mrs. Endycott. 'He might have lived longer, tho'.'

"Tis impossible to zay,' says Tom. 'Now, Jan's brither George, that's George Grant what used to farm Bittonwell; you remember 'en Mr. Annaferd fer certin; a black-muzzled feller with his two yers pokin' out each zide like a bat's wings, and his veet pointin' to quarter to dree, well, George never took much of a hand to cider. Tremenjis chap fer tay-drinkin', George was. Drink tay like a mothers' meetin', George wude. Use to carr' it out in the vields to-work, and Jan alwis declared it gived he the belly-ache to zee George abzorb tay like it. Well, and George took and died when he wad'n but a day or two over zixty, and Jan alwis use to zay 'twas becus his system did'n get proper nourishment.'

Mrs. Endycott said, 'Nobody id'n gwain to make me believe 'tis right thing vor any man to drink 'ight quarts o' cider a day. Do you think zo yerzell, Tom Zalter?'

'I don't think 'tis right vor he to have 'ight and me none, missis, if that's what you mean.'

'They zay cider is gude fer roomatics,' says Mrs. Snell.

'I believe 'tis right, too,' says Tom.

'You ab'm got roomatics, have 'ee?'

'I wude'n zay I've got roomatics now this very minute, Mrs. Snell, but I shude'n be at all surprised if I was to get a touch aw't when us comes to the Hoss and Jockey.'

'Well, you zay zo if you do, and I'm blest if you shan't have a drink o' cider fer once. I'll pay vor't mezell.'

The words wad'n spoke, hardly, bevore us yeard a most hawful groanin' back in the corner, and there was Lias Buzzacott with his two hands to the small of his back, and lookin' like anybody in draidful agony.

'Caw,' he says, 'I've got sitch a pain come in my back; stickin' in like a knive. Mus' be roomatics.'

Us was bound to laaf, and when us come to the Hoss and Jockey, Ned bought Lias a pint o' cider for his chick. Must have cured 'en, too, 'cus he did'n get no more roomatics, that journey.

'I can tell 'ee a li'l yarn about Jan Grant,' says Ned, 'and it mus' be twenty year agone fer certin. I met with 'n one day into Barleycombe——'

'Into the Rid Lion,' says Lias.

'No, it wad'n into the Rid Lion, young feller. What do you mean, Rid Lion! What shude I be doin' in the Rid Lion.'

'In the Angel,' says Lias again.

'No, it wad'n in the Angel, I tell 'ee. Do you think I'm in the habit o' gwain in they places.'

'Into the White 'Art.'

'Never you mind where 'twas to.'

'Guessed right third time,' says Lias. 'Go on, maister.'

'Be-as-'twill,' says Ned, 'I thought the ole feller was lookin' like as if he'd got zummin on his mind, so I axed 'n if he was worrittin' about aught.'

'"Not worrittin', Ned," he said. "I'm a bit puzzled, that's all."

'"What be puzzled about?" I said.

'"Well, 'tis like this-yer," he said. "You knaws Benjamin Dolebeer, the local praicher, daun' 'ee?"

'"I can't zay I don't know 'en, Jan," I said, "although I ban't very well acquainted with 'n, arter that. But what about 'n?"

'"Well," he says, "I use to meet with Benjamin a lot, one time, cus I use to buy pig-mail and sitch-like from 'en. And Benjamin was alwis praichin' me up sarments about the cider drinkin', and persuadin' me to jack it up."

'"'Twill be the death of 'ee, Jan Grant," he use to zay. "You'll be old man bevore your time, and 'twill kill 'ee bevore another ten years."

'"I'll bet 'ee zixpence it don't," I says.

'"I don't go in fer bettin', not as a rule," he says, "but I will bet 'ee zixpence this time, that if you goes on drinkin' the quantities o' cider, same's you be now, you'll be daid man bevore ten years, although you'm only zeb'm years older then I be. And when you do," he says, "I shall praiche a sarment to the chapel and tell the volks all about it, vor a warnin'."

'"That was ten year agone almost to the day, Mr. Annaferd," says Jan, "and I've drinked my peck o' cider every day, ever since."

'"Well, that's all right, Jan," I said. "You've winned the bet and 'tis your zixpence."

'"That's jus' what I'm puzzled about," he says.

'"I don't zee nothin' to be puzzled about, Jan," I said to 'en. "Benjamin made a bet with you that if you did'n stap drinkin' so much cider you'd be daid man in ten years. You didn' give up the cider, and you ab'm died, so what is there to puzzle about?"

'"Well, you zee," he says, "I've now returned from Bejamin's funeral, and I'm puzzled to know where I must send to, to get the zixpence."'

JAN BUILDS A HOUSE

1. THE PLANS

You'll often yer it said that a man don't know what he can do till he tries. I reckon that remark ought to be turned around tother way.

It shude be, a man don't know what he *can't* do till he tries.

There's heaps o' volks what thinks they cude do wonders if they liked. And they'll go on thinkin' it to the day o' their death, unless they shude hap'm to have a go at it; and then, most likely they'll vind out they ban't quite so clever as they thought they was.

'Tis amazin' how aisy 'tis to watch zome other body doin' a job and think you cude do it better. You zees how they goes to work and you thinks, 'Now, if that was me I shude do zo-an'-zo, and zo-an'-zo.'

As I zay, that's all very vine till you tries it. Any vule can get wonderful idayas in their mind, but wonderful idayas has a nasty 'abbit of gwain all wrong shape when you tries to fit 'em together and make 'em open and shut, or stand on vower legs, or hang up agin the wall. They looks very differ'nt when you brings 'em into sight to what they did when they was in yer mind.

I knaws all about it, 'cus I've had zome. I ban't spaikin' about other volks now; I'm spaikin' about mezell. And I ban't tellin this tale becus 'tis a pleasure to tell it. 'Tis no pleasure, I can assure 'ee, but if it shude be of assistance to anybody what thinks he id'n such a fule as he looks, 'twill be worth-a-while. If he can larn zummat at my expainse 'twill be chaiper than larnin' it at his awn.

When us had our houze done up inzide a bit agone, us had all new planchin' in the best rumes; or new floor-boards as towns-volks wude term it. The old boards which they tooked up was proper ratted in zome plaaces, but a lot aw'm was only jis' titched

97

at the ends, and zome was quite sound. So I had 'em putt back in a heap in the li'l yard, and there they bide for months.

One day my wive said, 'Pity all they boards shude lie there to waste. If us had up Dick Bradferd vor a couple o' days, he cude knack up a nice li'l shed with the gude parts. 'Tis a thing us cude do with very well to putt tools and sitch-like in.'

Now, if I'd had any sainse I'd have said, 'That's a very gude idaya. 'Tis Dick's trade and he'm the very chap to do it.'

But I did'n zay that. What I said was, 'What do us want to pay money to Dick Bradferd for? I cude putt up a shed as well as he; and a bit better, p'r'aps.'

'Don't talk so stoobid,' says Ann. 'What do you know about a job o' that sort? I don't want a eye-sore out in the yard.'

'What do 'ee mean, "eye-sore"?' I said. 'I'm tellin about a nice li'l shed, fit for anybody to zee.'

Her did'n zay no more, but the way her kep' quiet was a sight more annoyin' than the way her spoke. If you've bin married any length o' time you'll understand what I mean. So I thought to mezell, 'I'll let you zee I ban't such a fule as you thinks. If I cude'n do a li'l job like that 'tis a pity.'

Bless yer zaul, I cude zee it all done bevore I started. The idayas come into me mind as thick as a swarm o' bees.

'If I builds 'n up agin the wall,' I thought, 'that'll be one zide done bevore I starts. Then I only wants the corner uprights, and 'twill be cheel's play to nail a vew boards across. I'll let 'em zee about "eye-zore."'

That "eye-zore" business sticked in my droat, I can tell 'ee. I did'n intaind her to ferget that, and I was only lookin' vorrad to the time when her'd have to eat her words. After I'd started on the job, whenever mother come out and axed me what I was up to now, I told her I was gettin' on with the eye-zore. At laiste, I did vor the fust day or two, but after that I did'n zay it quite so much; and graj'ly I left it out altogether. However, I've got bevore my tale. I'll tell 'ee about that when I comes to it.

And now I'm gwain to tell you zummat, in case you did'n know it bevore. 'Tis one thing to have schemes in yer haid, but 'tis another thing altogether to putt 'em up in the back yard. If you'll remember that, it might zave 'ee from makin' such a fule o' yerzell as what I did. I had lovely plans in me haid, and better-fit I'd let 'em bide there.

It all looked so aisy, too. There was the boards, and there was the space to putt up the shed. All I required was a 'ammer and a vew nails. The more I considered it, the bigger my idayas did become.

'Never mind about a shed,' I said to mother. 'I'll make it a proper li'l houze while I'm about it, with a winder to one end, where us can store away all manner o' things. And I'll fix up shelves all around so's you can have a plaace fer yer odds and ainds. You shan't complain no more about not havin' a out-houze like other women.'

So I tooked off me coat and sot to work.

Fust thing was to have the zaw and cut out all the good bits in they boards. A wretched nuisance that was, 'cus you veeled you was wastin' a lot o' time, and gettin' the back-ache most jewsive, but you wad'n makin' no headway with the job. That's when I fust beginned to railise the differ'nce between havin' plans and fulfillin' 'em. You zay to yerzell, 'Fust of all I'll jis' cut out the gude bits o' board,' and in your mind that job's finished. But 'tis a very differ'nt matter when you comes to carr' it out. Took me a couple o' days' hard work to zaw up that 'ude, and long bevore I'd vinished I was zick and tired o' the zight of it.

Mind, I cude have done it a lot quicker if I cude have gone me awn way to work, and mother had'n come interfering. Not that I wants to make out me awn way was the best, 'cus 'twad'n. I'm willin' to admit that now, although I wad'n at the time.

You'd think any fule cude cut up a vew boards, wude'n 'ee. But 'tid'n so aisy as you might think, not when you'm gwain to build a houze with 'en. I'd zawed up 'ude bevore, many's a times, but 'twas only rough and ready, jis' to burn in the vire. So it did'n matter if 'twas a trifle out o' the straight. And I was doin' this job the zame till my Ann come out to zee what her cude vind fau't with.

'Why daun' 'ee cut 'em square?' her says.

'What do 'ee mean? I be cuttin' 'em square, ban't I?'

'Of coorse you ban't. Look at the one you've jis' cut off. Do you call he'm square?'

'Cert'nly he is. 'Tis your eye that's out o' truth.'

'Aw, is it?' her says. 'Well, you putt two ends together and zee.'

So her putt two ends o' boards together, and I'm jiggered if you cude'n get a pound o' cheese in between. I tried to make out her wad'n holdin' the boards straight.

'All right,' her said, 'lie 'em one tap tother, and zee how they'll agree.'

They did'n agree at all. I knowed very well they wad'n gwain
to.

'Git out,' I said, 'you'm too finickin' by half. It won't make all
that odds if the ends ban't zac'ly straight.'

But her wude'n have that.

'Purty vine houze that'll be,' her says, 'with the ends gwain in
and out like a flight o' staps. Why ever did'n you have a straight
edge and make a line across, so's you cude zee where to go to?'

Of coorse, if I'd gived it a thought, that's what I shude 'a-done.
'Twas vexin' that mother shude point it out, but anybody cude
zee 'twas right. So after that I had a straight-edge and a bit o'
pencil and marked it out proper.

But makin' a mark id'n everything. I be dal'd if 'tis. You've got
to volley the mark arter you've made it, and unless a feller have
done a bit to it, 'tid'n alwis so aisy. Once you begins to get away
from the line 'tis impossible to get back, and the furder you goes
the wiss you be. And sure as ever I got a bit off the mark, mother
wude come out to watch, and keep tellin' me I wad'n gwain
straight. 'Tis no wonder I said things I did'n ought to.

"Tis no gude you lostin' yer temper,' her says. 'I be only tellin'
'ee for yer awn gude.'

However, I got more accustomed to it arter a bit o' practise.
Presen'ly mother hap'm to come out when I was dree parts o' the
way droo a board, and I wad'n a hair's-breadth off the mark.

'What about this one?' I said, and I vinished 'n right across,
daid on the line.

'You've got 'n straight nuff,' her said, 'but you ab'm got 'n
square.'

'What be talkin' about now?'

'Neether you ab'm. You don't keep yer zaw upright. 'Tis all
slopin' away in under.'

Darned if her wad'n right. There was no gettin' away from it.
'Twas more like the edge of a chisel than the edge of a board.

'A li'l thing like that id'n gwain to make no odds,' I said. But I
cude zee 'twas gwain to mean trouble when I come to fit two
boards together.

And that's the sort o' thing a feller don't anticipate when he
tells about doin' this, that and tother. They crops up as you goes
along and upzets all your vine schemes. It larns 'ee not to rin
away with the idaya that another chap's job is as aisy as it looks.

But that was only the beginning. I had heaps more to larn yet.

I won't zay I was sick o' me job bevore I'd properly started. I won't go so fur as to zay that. But I'll tell 'ee what I will zay. Bevore I was half-ways droo with it I wished with all me 'art I had'n made such a zong about what I was gwain to do bevore I started to do it.

And that's my advice to anybody what thinks of takin' on a job he id'n accustomed to. Wait till you zees what it looks like when 'tis vinished and then zay that's how you intainded it to be. Nobody can't contrydict 'ee then. But if you makes up a long ole rigmarole bevore you starts, about the wonderful things you'm gwain to prevorm, you'm only axin' vor trouble. You won't get no praise fer the part you do's right; only radicule for what you do's wrong.

I made the mistaake of describin' what my houze was gwain to look like when 'twas vinished, bevore I'd begun on 'en. Therefore they was able to compare the one I had in my mind with the one I left up agin the wall. And I may as well tell 'ee straight out, they wad'n very much alike.

Mind you, 'tid'n so bad as all that. I wude'n call it a eye-sore, mezell. And mother, her did'n zay 'twas eye-sore, neether, 'cus I axed her the ques'ion, straight out. I said, 'You wude'n call that a eye-sore, now wude 'ee?'

And her did'n zay 'twas. Her said:

'Depends on which way you looks at it.'

And that's quite true. It do make a differ'nce which way you views it. Walkin' out from the back door it don't look so bad, 'cus the dairy pokes out and hides it a bit, and so you come on to it gradjule, like. 'Tis when you comes in droo the gaate and gets it full butt, all to one glimpse. That's when it tries 'ee a bit.

But 'tis wonderful how you can get used even to a thing like that. I can pass in and out now, and not take very much notice of it. But in the case o' strangers, I likes for 'em to go in the front way and out droo the kitchen. It breaks the news more gentle, as the sayin' is.

Furthermore, you can't get away from the fact that 'tis useful. Us have got sevver'l things stored inzide there which used to be exposed to the rain a lot more than what they be now. But still, takin' one thing with another, and lookin' at it all the way round, I wude'n zay, on the whole, if a gurt weend was to come in the night and blaw down the whole contraption but what 'twude be a mercy. I shude think, by the look of it, that's what'll happen in the end.

But I'm bevore my tale again. I'm tellin' about the place comin' down bevore I've told 'ee how it got putt up.

2. THE FINISHED ARTICLE

I got the blessid ole timber cut up to-last, but it took me a lot longer than I ordained. That's what I vound with most o' the jobs. I'd 'low half-a-nower, and 'twude take me half a day.

Like the nex' job I done; puttin' in the paustis. I thought to mezell:

'I'll jis' dig down vower holes in the vower cornders and putt in they uprights, and that'll break the back aw't.'

But I'm jiggered if it did'n nearly break mine. The ground had'n bin disturbed fer hunderds o' years, I don't suppose, and 'twas like diggin' iron, zac'ly. 'Twas full o' gurt stones, about two to a barra-load, and time I'd done me vower holes I cude 'a-buried vower sheep, purt' near. However, I reckoned the wist o' me troubles was over when I'd dug they holes. I was alwis makin' that mistaake. Every job I done I thought that was the wist, and then I vound the next was wisser still.

'Now to get up they vower uprights,' I said. "Twill be nort then to nail the boards across.'

You'd think any fule cude stick vower paustis upright, wude'n 'ee? But I vound one fule that cude'n.

I putt the fust paust up agin the wall, and that wad'n so bad, 'cus there was zummat to stay 'en. I got 'n what I considered was upright, and putt in a vew stones and a bit of airth to keep 'n in plaace, and then I sot about the one oppozyte. He had'n got no support, so I had to trist to me eye to get he vitty. That was a turk of a job, that was, 'cus every time I rammed down a stone or two, to make'n safe, I'd push 'en out o' the straight. When I stepped back to have another look, I'd vind he'd gone over wan way or tother. He very near drove me mazed, he did.

You zee, where I was a stoobid, and I railized it when 'twas too laate, I wude'n let mother 'sist me as her wanted to. When her

zee'd I was about to get on with the paustis, her said, 'You'd
better wait a minute, 'genst I've washed up these vew things, and
then I'll come and lend 'ee a hand. You'll require zomebody to
hold up they paustis while you gets 'em straight.'

Truth o' the matter was, her'd got a lot more sainse to look
ahaid than what I had, only I had'n got the gumtion to know it. I
thought to mezell, 'You wants to be able to zay arterwards that I
cude'n putt up the houze without your help.'

'So I said, 'You look arter your jobs indoors. I'll manage this all
right. Pity if I can't stick a paust in the ground without a wumman
assistin' me.'

All very well for me to talk like that. Sounded very big, I
dersay, but 'twad'n very long bevore I wished I had'n been
hardly so rash. I cude'n very well ax her to come out and help
now, after spaikin' to her that fashin, and there wad'n no other
body I cude call upon. But I verily did think they uprights wude
drive me to distraction.

As I zay, I got the second one there of thereabouts, and then I
putt tother feller agin the wall, which wad'n no gurt criterion. So
now there was only one more left. But he'd got to match two
ways; and do you think I cude make 'n do it? He was as stubborn
as pig. If I got 'n right with the wan behind he'd be all wrong with
one oppozyte, and when I putt 'n straight with that one he'd be
all skew-wiff with tother. I shude never have believed it was
possible for vower bits of 'ude to behave so contr'y. I'd stand out
in front and get 'em lookin' a bit thereafter. Then I'd walk around
to get the sideways view and they'd be all over the shop. I tried
every way to make 'em look right in each derection and to-last I
got out of all patience with 'em and I said, 'Well, if you won't go
in the right plaace you must bide in the vicinity, that's all, and one
mus' counterac' tother. What's over at the top must come off at
the bottom, and nobody won't notice a li'l thing like that when
I've nailed the boards across.'

I'd got vower paustis up, anyway, even if they did'n agree,
zac'ly, and I went fullin' in the holes quick, bevore mother cude
come out and start to critickise. I won't zay they was up as I'd
pictured they wude be, and I must admit they lookid a zight
more as if they got there by accident than been putt there
a-purpose. Any stranger wude be more likely to think 'twas a old
houze comin' down than a new one puttin' up. But I'd got to that

state when I was beginnin' to be thankful for small mercies. I'd decided it wude'n do to be too pa'ticler, if the job was ever gwain to be finished at all. And what with diggin' they ole pits and messin' about with the uprights, I was achin' in every joint.

However, I stumped down the airth and stones around the paustis, and zac'ly as I'd finished out come mother.

'Ullaw,' her saith, 'your troubles is just about to begin, I zee.'

'That shows you can zee a vat lot,' I says. 'I shude zay they'm just about to end.'

'Aw, wude 'ee? You'll never be able to fasten boards to they uprights. You ab'm got 'em square.'

'They ban't so very fur out, not if you come over yer and look.'

'I'm not spaikin' about the uprightness. You've got 'em twested. Carry over a board and I'll show 'ee what I mean.'

But I zee'd what her meaned in a minute. I'd bin so intent on gettin' they paustis upright, I had'n bothered about havin' the flat zides all lookin' the zame derection. When us held a board flush agin one upright he wude'n come within a voot or eighteen inches o' the next one, and if us putt 'n flat agin both the paustis he only titched the very corners, where no nail wude ever hold 'n. I tried to make out it did'n make no odds, but mother wude'n have it.

'You can't nail boards to the uprights as they be,' her saith, 'that's a very sure thing. You shude have took care they was square when you putt 'em in.'

'A chap can't think of everything,' I says.

'Well, you'll have to start thinkin' about zome of 'em. The only thing to do is to dig away they uprights and twest 'em around straight. Or else let 'em bide as they be and hang up a clothes-line to 'em. They'd come in very handy that way.'

Any fule cude zee that what her said was right. I tried to vind zome way out aw't, but 'twas no gude. I had to do as her said. Then I had a long board and nailed across the front down the bottom, and a short one each end.

''Tis beginnin' to look a bit ship-shape now the walls be gwain up,' I said.

'Where be gwain to put the chumley to?' says mother.

'Daun' be redeclus, with yer chumley.'

'Daun't you be redeclus. If you'm gwain to nail boards all around you'll have to have a chumley to climb down to get inzide.'

104

Darn me, I'd fergot all about the door for the minute.

'That's you, keepin' on so,' I said. 'I did'n mean to putt a board all along that end, 'cus I be gwain to have a door there.'

'Where shall 'ee get a door to?'

'Shall have to make one, I reckon. 'Twaun't take very much to knack up a door.'

'No, and I daun't expec' 'twill take very much to knack 'n down again arter he'm up.'

'He'll be all right,' I says. 'Daun' you worry.'

'Twas all very well to tell about puttin' up a door, but 'twad'n so simple when I come to look close at it. Fer one thing, it meant puttin' up another paust, 'cus o' coorse, I had'n got nort to hang 'n to. 'Twude 'a-bin all right if I'd only sot out to putt up a rough and raddy plaace. But I'd made up so much ole palarver about what my houze was gwain to look like that I beginned to get proper frightened when I zee'd what shape he was gwain up. And I knowed, the more uprights I had to putt in, the more shapes he was gwain to be.

When I started, I ordained puttin' a winder in one end, but I'd gived up that projec' long ago. Mother come out again while I was tryin' to induce the upright to bide in his plaace. 'I wonder what 'twill be this time,' I thought to mezell.

'I can't think,' her says, 'why you don't tack a piece across the top o' they uprights to keep 'em in plaace.'

'I was jus' thinkin' whether that wude'n be the better way or no,' I said.

'Twas lies. I never thought no-sitch thing, but I cude zee in a minute 'twas right. I nailed a rap across the top and then I did'n have half the trouble.

So then I boarded up the short side where there wad'n gwain to be no door, to help keep the uprights firm. Twad'n no turrable bad, only I did'n get the bottom one properly level, so the boards was all to a slin as they went up. You wude'n notice it very much unless you lookid straight at 'em, but o' coorse, mother detected it in a minute.

'Nobody id'n gwain to stap a gallopin' hoss to zee that,' I said. And mother said they wude'n need to. However, I got that side all fulled up, with exception of a bit o' space one end up the top, where the last board wude'n come egzacly vitty. 'That'll do for ventilation,' I said.

'Strikes me,' says mother, 'ventilation is gwain to be the best thing about it. I dunnaw that you'll need to trouble about a door, after all. There'll be heaps o' places to go in and out.'

But I was no sooner out from one quandairy than I was into another. 'Twas mother again.

'What be gwain to putt across the front?' her says.

'What do 'ee think I be gwain to putt, strips o' paaper?'

''Twill need to be zummin' o' the sort, 'cus there id'n more 'n two o' they boards will stretch all the way across.'

My dear zaul, I veeled like pickin' up the biggest thing I cude find and scattin' the whole consarn all to flibbits. To think I had'n had the gumtion to measure things a bit bevore I started.

'The only thing,' I says, 'is to use two short ones in place o' one long one.'

'How be gwain to do that, when you ab'm got nothin' to nail 'em to. You'll have to putt up another upright in the middle.'

Another upright! My dear life. Another hole in the ground. More back-ache. But there was no other way out aw't.

This time mother putt a hand to the paust, so it wad'n so ockerd. Of coorse, her dunnaw nothin' about buildin' a houze, but if I told her what to do her cude hold up the upright while I went back and took a glimpse at 'n to get 'n straight. The I'd hold 'n while her went back to look, and that wude putt the finishin' touch. Her'd sure to zay I was a bit out, and make me alter 'n a trifle. But I let her have her awn way. I was got to such a pitch by thees time, all I wanted was to zee the blessid thing finished. It hadn' turned out a bit like I meant for it to, and once a thing like that starts bein' ockerd, the furder you goes the wiss it gets.

Us got the front boarded up, some sort o' fashin, and if you stood fur 'nuff back you cude 'n zee a gurt lot the matter wai't. And us done up the zide, with exception of a hole fer' the door. By that time I'd bin messin' about egzac'ly a wik, and I was thankful 'nuff fer Zindy to come and give me a day's rest. I did'n go out in back yard any more than I cude help.

Mondy I started on makin' a door; and that shows I had'n larned me lesson even yet. I thought any fule cude make a door. And p'r'aps I was right. Anyway, if you was to zee my door I don't doubt for one instant but what you'd zay zome fule done it. However, he stops up most o' the hole, and he'll open and shut if you knaws the proper way to work 'en.

106

And as fer the roof, the least us says about that one the better. He have got a roof; and that's more than I thought he was gwain to have, one time. As my Ann says, if her only keeps the things in the shed which won't spoil in the wet, he'll come in handy.

But I wude'n call it a eye-sore. And Lias Buzzacott said the zame. He said he wude'n call it a eye-sore, 'cus I axed 'n that very ques'ion.

'Lias,' I said, 'now spaik the truth. You wude'n call thikky shed a eye-sore, wude 'ee?'

And he said, 'No, maister. I wude'n call it a eye-sore. But I know scores o' people what wude.'

THE MAN WHO LOST HIS MEMORY

1.   ALFY DISPIN'S BRAIN-WAVE

Alfy Dispin was a li'l small man with a big wife. They lived in the cottage that stands by itzelf, down bottom end o' the village. There was two things in this world that prevented Alfy from bein' properly happy; one was his wife that I've jis' mentioned, and tother was work. If he had'n had to go to work when he went out, and if he had'n had to give account of it to his wife when he come in, life would 'a-bin worth livin' for 'en.

What wude have suited he best would be, whenever he went out to go to the Rid Lion, and when he come home to sit and rade the newspaper. Both they jobs suited Alfy right down to the ground. The trouble was, his missis did'n think very much of eether of 'em, and Lucy Dispin's thinkin' had a lot more to do with Alfy's comin's and goin's than his awn. Theirs was one of the homes where the hen done the crawing.

The consequence was, although Alfy was so fond o' gwain to the Rid Lion, he did'n have very much of what you go to Rid Lions with. So he got in the habit of havin' his drinks putt up on the slate. That was all very well for a time, but one aiv'min the lan'lord told 'n he'd lost the pencil and had'n got no more room on the slate, so he cude'n let Alfy have no more beer till he'd paid the back-lash.

That was a draidful state of affairs, 'cus it meant that Alfy had to spend a lot more time harkening to his wife's opinion aw'n; and he knawed it all off by 'art. He was one o' those men whose wives daun' appreciate their gude qualities. Her knawed all his bad ones and cude rattle 'em off wai'out stoppin' fer breath. But Alfy veeled he was misunderstood. He reckoned if he was to die, her'd railise his gude points and wish her had 'n back again, so's her cude trate 'n better. The worst o' bein' dead was, it lasted

108

sitch a long time, and he wude'n get the benevit of her bein' sorry for all her domineerin' ways. If 'twas only possible to die fer a bit and then come back to life again, 'twude be worth-a-while, jus' to let her zee what her was missin'.

The idaya come to 'en wan day all in a flash. He'd jus' bin raidin' another account on the paper of a chap what had lost his memory and cude'n remember nothing. That was the third case he'd come across in about a vortnit. The details was purty much the zame every time. A chap wude go out about his business as usual, and all of a sudden he'd be lost. The next thing they'd yer of 'n, he'd be wanderin' about in zome strange plaace and cude'n remember a thing; not even his awn name and derections. Then he'd be took every care of and putt to bed, p'raps in a hospital, and have nice nourishin' vood and wine, and be cawdled up in hopes his memory wude come back. And, o' coorse, he did'n have to do no work, 'cus lostin' the memory is a turrable strain, so he had to rest a lot.

Restin' was a job that Alfy took to like a duck takes to watter. 'Twas the best thing Alfy cude do, rest.

And, o' coorse, all the time the feller was missin', his wife was in a draidful way about 'n, seekin' all over the plaace, and wishin' her'd traited 'n better while her had 'n, and makin' up her mind of all the nice things her'd do vor 'en if only her cude get 'n back. Alfy thought hard fer a long time and then he said to hiszelf:

'I cude do it. I cude lost me memory. Why cude'n I? 'Tis only to ferget everything, and that's zac'ly what I wants to do. I cude ferget all they figures on the slate. If I was found wanderin' about in zome strange plaace with me memory all gone, they'd be glad nuff to rub 'em out and stand me drinks. I'll do it.'

So he stidded all the pa'ticlers in the cases on the papers, to know zac'ly how to go to work, and then he started on his venter.

The fus' thing to do was to get a long distance away from where he belonged to. They all done that, and o' coorse he must be vound by perfec' strangers. They'd be more likely to take pity on 'en than the volks what knowed 'en well; and he must be missin' as long as possible bevore they discovered his whereabouts. The longer he was lost the more time his wife wude have to repent for her hard'artedness.

'Twas jist on vive o' clock when Alfy started off. 'Twas a winter's aiv'min and jis comin' in nice and dark, so nobody see'd the gwain aw'n. He left his 'at and coat behind, hanged up, so's to make it look more railastic. He durzen travel on the rawds, o' coorse, 'cus it wude'n do to meet with anybody what knawed 'n. He had to cut across the vields the best way he cude, and creep droo all manner o' dark plaaces. 'Twad'n very pleasant, 'cus the grass was wet, and 'twas mortle cold in his shirt-sleeves, with no 'at. And poking about in the dark like he was, he keeped on gettin' in the zugs; so 'twad'n very long bevore his veet was wet as muck.

If he'd bin forced to take such a journey in the ordinary way o' business, he'd have kicked up a middlin' vine ole shindy. But his thoughts was all tooked up with what was gwain to be the outcome aw't, and that keeped his 'art up. He cude'n help o' laafin' when he picshered what wude hap'm. Zoon arter he'd left the houze his missis wude be gettin' the tay. Then her'd go to the back door and give a shout for'n, as if her was callin' the dog. Wan shout was sufficient as a rule, 'cus the nex' best thing Alfy was gude at bezides resting was his meals. Then he cude zee her gettin' up and shoutin' the second time, and 'twude be zome shout, begad, 'cus her did'n relish havin' to call twice for 'en. 'Twude start all the hens cackling in the parish. When her'd waited another vive minutes and still he did'n turn up, what uproar there wude be to be sure. Her'd finish her awn tay quick, and then putt away all the things, determined to tell'n that if he cude'n come to his meals proper time he cude go without.

As the time went on and he did'n appear her wude imagine he'd gone up to the pub, drinking. Her'd snatch up her 'at, and putt'n on as if her was gwain to pull it right down round her neck, and off-do-go to the Rid Lion, to march him home before the eyes of everybody.

When her found he was'n there, and nobody had'n zee'd 'en her'd begin to rack her brains to think what caper he was on upon. And what a speech her'd be gettin' ready for'n, 'genst he did come home to-last. Alfy nearly laafed out loud, cold as he was.

Then 'twude knock along to bed time, and still no Alfy. By that time her'd hardly be able to contain herself. Her'd leave off thinking what her was gwain to say and start thinking what her was gwain to do.

But as hour arter hour went by her'd begin to wonder what cude have happened, and whether he had'n had a accident or no. It almost made li'l Alfy veel warm to picsher his wife rinnin' around to the neighbours to know if they'd yeard aught of her husband or no. Then o' coorse, they'd all take it up and the news wude begin to spread about.

'By that time her'll begin to wish her had'n bin hardly so rash with her tongue,' Alfy thought to hiszelf; 'and bim-bye her'll get that anxious, her'll go right off to the policeman's. Then the fun will begin proper. Policeman will ride on his bicycle to the differ'nt plaaces where I might be to, but everywhere 'twill be the zame tale. Nobody ab'm zee'd me, nor yeard a word o' me. When he goes back and reports that to mother her'll be in a turrable way. And waun't her wish her cude take back zome o' the bad names her've called me. Waun't her just!

'Then they'll waken up all the men in the village, and there'll be a proper human-cry. They'll all go zeeking vor me with lighted lanterns. And nex' mornin' 'twill all be on the paper.'

That was the part Alfy liked to think about most; his name in big letters up the head o' the cullum, and then a long ole rigmarole all about 'en. It had never happened to any other body in the parish excep' Jim Davey when he had a fight with the keeper. Of coorse, that was a very differ'nt thing, and not very much to his credit. The only thing Alfy was vexed about was, he did'n zee how he cude very well buy a paper, when he come to a town, without givin' hiszelf away.

'They'll do a big trade out about thase parts,' he thought to hiszelf. 'Everybody will buy a paper to rade about the mysterious disappearance of Alfy Dispin. They'll print my discription and what togs I had on, and the colour o' me hair; and they can't deny but what I be a good-lookin' chap. Everybody will lef' work to-morra and go furragin' about in every copse and vuz-brake in the neighbourhood. They'll poke in the straimes and let out all the ponds to zee if Alfy Dispin's body is down bottom. But it will be many miles away by that time.

'Ees, and when 'tis railised that I be lost, and p'raps died a hawful death, all they what have spoke coose about me will alter their chune. They'll zay, "Us was too hard on the poor feller, keeping on 'You owes me this,' and 'When be you gwain to pay me that?' If 'twude only bring 'n back to life us wude forgive 'n all his debts and welcome."

'They'll zay it to my missis, fer certin; so her'll be able to bear witness to it when I be took back with me memory all gone. I

111

shall be discovered miles away from home wanderin' about starvin' hungerd and tired as a dog, not knowin' where I've come from nor where I be gwain to. When they ax me my name I shall look at 'em strange, and won't be able to tell 'em. Then they'll zay, "The poor feller have lost his memory. He mus' be took care of."

'I only hope I shall be vound by zomebody a bit thereafter, who will trait me up to the mark. I must try to manage that, and not be picked up by any Dick, Tom or 'Arry. They'll think, "P'raps this is the poor chap whose name have been on the paper." So then they'll zend for Lucy to come and identify me. But I shan't know her from Adam. I shan't recognise her no more than if her was a perfec' stranger. And I dunnaw yet how long I shall let pass bevore I *do* recognise her. I shall wait and zee how things goes on first.'

Such thoughts as thase helped Alfy along as he trapesed on mile arter mile in the dark. But after he'd thought 'em all over a time or two they did'n answer the purpose so well. They beginned to lose their strength. You zee, they was only thoughts after all, but the hedges and ditches, and the zugs and the brimmles, and the things that kep' knacking up agin his head was all real. When he stepped in a straime up to his knees in watter, or ketched zome part of hiszelf on a gurt thorn, a differ'nt sort o' thoughts come into his mind and drove the nice ones out. Once when he was pushin' his way droo a hole in a hedge, hopin' to vind a path o' zome zort t'other zide, he putt his hand right in a spring trap. All the memory-losting in the world won't make 'n ferget what that was like. 'Twas a wonder he had'n broke every bone in his vingers, and for a bit he thought he had. He cude veel they was bliddin' though 'twas too dark to zee what he'd done to hiszelf.

When he hanged up his coat bevore he lef' home he fergot to take his pipe and baccy and matches out from the pocket, so he cude'n have a smauk. 'Twude have helped him on considerable if he cude have had a smauk. And by thees time I'm jiggered if he cude'n have done with a bit of helpin'. The furder he went the harder job he had to keep his sperrits up. He had'n got no more idaya where he was to, than the man in the mune. Ner he had'n got the faintest notion what time 'twas. The only thing he knawed was it mus' be zomewhere about zupper time. When he thought

112

about his zupper he groaned in sperrit; or not in sperrit egsac'ly, but in the place where he felt hungry to.

And he thought he'd never felt so hungry bevore in his life. He'd started off without his tay, and now he was properly leery. He tried to think about his name bein' on the paper in big letters, but that did'n do nort towards fillin' his stomach.

However, when he got over the next hedge he come out into a bit of a lane, and then he reckoned he knowed where he was to. He cude make out a stonen wall t'other zide the rawd, and he considered he cude own the place.

'That's Farmer Brimmlecombe's wall, to Draycott, fer a bet of a guinea. Jis' fancy me bein' all out yer. I've come furder than I thought I had. I ban't such a turrable long way from Nackaburge. I'll clim' up auver the wall, and then if I flip across the coort I can get out into the turnpike. I shan't meet nobody there thees time o' night, fer certain, and I shall be able to get along half as fast again.'

So Alfy climmed up the wall, arter a deal o' trouble. 'Twas higher than he thought. If it had'n bin fer a stone pokin' out jis' the right heighth for 'n to putt his voot on, he'd never got up at all.

'Shows how aisy anybody can be desayved,' he said to hiszelf. 'If anybody had axed me I shude 'a-bet any money that Farmer Brimmlecombe's wall was'n no more'n vive feet high; but he mus' be handier zeb'm, fer certin.'

However, he got up 'pon top and then lowered hiszelf down t'other zide till he was only hangin' on by his vingers. It never occurred to 'en till 'twas too laate that he wude'n be able to reach the ground. So there he was stretchin' down with his toes, but o' coorse, they wude'n titch nothin'. 'Twas a turrable ockerd quandairy to be in, and if he cude have pulled hiszelf up again he wude have; but he wad'n man enough for that. Furthermore he cude'n bide hanging very long, cus his vingers was all cripped with the trap. 'Twas the fus' time Alfy had bin properly warm since he left home, and now he was rinnin' down in straimes o' sw'atting.

'Never mind,' he thought to hiszelf. ''Tis only a couple o' veet at the outzide. There can't be very much to hurt in that short distance.'

He was right. There wad'n. He let go and went down. Fer the fus' two veet there wad'n nothin'; and not very much the next vower. Nothin' to stand on, anyway. Alfy expected his veet to stap with a bump, but they did'n. They jis' went on, and when they did stop he was up to the neck in watter.

He'd gone plop in the deep end o' the pond.

The shock to Alfy's system was so tremenjis that he fergot which end was his head, and that end went down the bottom of the icy cold watter. Bevore it come up again he'd swallered as much as most men wude use to wash theirzel's in. When he got back his speech he started to discribe his veelin's. 'Twas a long discription, and lasted till he reached the edge o' the pond and all the time the watter was rinnin' out of his shirt sleeves and down the ligs of his trousers. He had'n lost his memory up to then, that's a certin sure thing, cus he remembered all the things he'd ever been told not to zay; and he said 'em all over twice.

When he come partly back to his sainses the fus' thing he railised was that he wad'n in Farmer Brimmlecombe's, cus he knowed there wad'n no pond to Draycott. The nex' thing he railised was the he did'n know no more'n a cat where he was to, ner how he was gwain to get away from it. But the thing he railised most of all was that the weend was blawin' right straight droo 'en, and his teeth was chitterin' to such extent he cude'n yer hiszelf think. He was so bewildered that when he did start to move he walked back into the watter.

He turned around and scammled off in that oppozyte derection with his hands out in front to avoid bangin' into zummin hard, and hopin' to gudeness he wude'n go down a hole or waken the dog. By gude luck he rinned slap into the gaate, and got out in a vield. Fer two peens he'd have gived up his memory-losting and knacked to the farm door, only he cude'n think of any excuse for bein' there that time o' night, or mornin', or whatever 'twas. So he continued his journey over hedges and ditches, hopin' every time twude be the turnpike tother zide. And to-last it was.

When Alfy veeled his veet on the rawd he started to rin so's to get back a bit o' warmth into his sytem. But to make matters wiss, zummat started to vall. 'Twad'n rain, zac'ly, and 'twad'n snaw, and 'twad'n hail. 'Twas a sort of mixture of all dree, and it zeemed as if every drap went in one zide and out tother.

Presen'ly he said to hiszelf, 'I wonder if I be fur nuff from home to lost me memory? If I thought I was I'd vind zome-place where there was a bit o' shelter and lie down and go to sleep.'

THE MAN WHO LOST HIS MEMORY

When he started out Alfy thought he knowed all the rules, but it had'n turned out like he ordained. Like a good many things else, it zeemed aisy nuff when you planned it all out in yer mind, but 'twas a very differ'nt matter when you come to zet about it.

'If I knawed what time 'twas,' he thought, 'I shude have zome idaya how fur I'd come.' With the zame, a church clock started to strike zomewhere in the distance.

'*Dong!*'

'Gude! One o'clock. Eight howers I've bin trav'lin.'

'*Dong!*'

'Better still. Two o' clock. I must have gone——'

'*Dong!*'

Dree, begad! Better an' better.'

'*Dong!*'

'Vower o' clock! Alfy, you'm in——'

'*Dong!*'

All of a sudden he railised what was the matter. He was cold nuff bevore, gudeness knows, but now he turned into stone. He knowed what was gwain to hap'm. 'Twas gwain to go on donging, and the night had'n passed away so much as he thought.

And zo it did. Alfy counted every stroke, prayin' each time there'd be one more dong, and 'fraid of his life there wude'n be. He counted up to nine, and that was the last. He waited and waited, and held his breath, and harkened with all his yers. But he never listened to sitch hawful silence in his life.

Only nine o' clock! Only vower howers! If anybody had said vower years he wude'n have been surprised. Dree more such ages to go droo bevore he cude be lost and vound. Wet, cold, and as leery as a drum. He sot down bezide the rawd and fer a time he was as miserable as 'twas possible fer anybody to be. Losting the memory wad'n half so aisy as anybody wude think. Then he beginned to cheer up a bit.

'Arter all,' he thought to hiszelf, 'I've bin gwain vower howers, so I've got a tidy way. Suppausin' I've only travelled two mile a nower, that's eight miles. Zome volks what has lost their memory hasn't travelled much furder than eight mile, I don't expect. Now I be on a gude rawd I can aisy do another eight. That'll be zixteen, and I reckon that's fur enough.'

So he started off again in better sperrits. Presen'ly he passed by zummin white bezide the rawd.

'A derectin' paust. Now I shall know where I be to.'

'Twas too dark to zee what was on it, so he had to clim' right up to the tap. Alfy id'n much of a hand for that sort of caper, so it took 'n a turrable long time to clim' up. But comin' down was the quickest thing he ever done in his life. Matter o' fac', he zimply let go to the paust and come down in all one jit. He picked hiszelf up and then dragged slowly across the rawd, hopin' and prayin' he wude'n vind a post-box in the wall to the corner.

The post-box was there.

Alfy was about two gun-shots from his awn cottage.

2.   JIM DAVEY TAKES A HAND

I must let Alfy bide to the cross-rawds for a bit, while I go back and let 'ee know what had bin gwain on, all this time in his awn home.

Alfy had had it all planned out in his mind what was gwain to hap'm, and what his missis was gwain to do, and the policeman, and the sarchin' party and all the rest aw't. But how often do things turn out as us surmises they'm gwain to?

It started all right, jist as Alfy foretold it would. But it had'n gone very fur bevore it rinned right off the track. Lucy Dispin got her husban's tay as usual, and her went to the back door to shout, jist as he picshered it. And that's as fur as he guessed right.

Two things happened to cause the story to go all 'thurt after that. Fust of all, Mrs. Dispin did'n lay tay fer herself, only fer Alfy; and second of all, Jim Davey happened to be creepin' along in under the hedge down bottom of Alfy's garden, fer a short cut into Squire Manning's copse; where he hoped to vind zummat suitable for nex' Zindy's dinner.

Jim Davey's a gude-fer-nothin', pauchin' rascal, what never took nothing out of his reach, and wude zooner scheme all day to get a meal that do one hour's work for it. And yet fer all that, a chap very well liked by everybody excep' they what had got more than they was intitled to, in Jim's estimation. He used to reckon he was doing that sort a kindness, by making gude use of what wude go to waste else.

Be-as-'twill, he was just on his way to make gude use of one of Squire's spare burds, or a rabbut, or whatever come along, when

Mrs. Dispin putt her head out the door and holleyed:

'Alfy!'

Jim cruckied down and stood still as a stonen gaate-paust, waitin' to zee where Alfy wude answer from. But Alfy did'n answer from nowhere, 'cus by thees time he was off on his memory-losing caper. So missis holleyed again, and putt a bit more ginger behind it.

'Al-FAY!'

Jim cude imitate anybody's voice, 'speshly a squaiky li'l one like Alfy's, so he answered bak: 'Ullaw!'

Lucy was properly desayved.

'Take the stuffin' out o' yer ears, and not make me shout twice,' her says. And then her went on:

'Harken yer! I've left your tay all ready on the table and you can come and get it so-soon as you've got the muck off your boots. Tid'n gude you makes any mud-marks on the floor. I'm gwain up to have a dish o' tay with Mrs. Blissit as I promised her. I shall be home again 'long about zeb'm o' clock, so don't you go out bevore I gets back, mind.'

'Or-right, my dear,' says Jim, in Alfy's voice, zac'ly.

Jim peeped droo the hedge, and by the light in the kitchen winder he zee'd Mrs. Dispin come out the door with her 'at and coat on, and go out the rawd gaate. He laafed to hiszel' as he squaised droo the hedge into the garden.

"Twude be pity to let that nice tay spoil,' he said to hiszel'. 'There's no knowin' how long Alfy might be.'

He flipped up droo the garden into the kitchen, and barred the door behind 'en. That wude give 'n another minute or two in case of accidents, like Mrs. Dispin lookin' back for her hank'cher, or aught like o' that. Alfy's comin' he did'n mind in the laiste. He was willin' to meet any man, but he was feared of his life of a wumman. He lookid round the kitchen.

'This is zummin like,' he says. 'Butiful gurt vire and a tay fit for a king. Jim Davey, you did'n expec' two boiled aigs, braid 'n butter, a gurt slishe o' plum caake and a pot o' tay to waish it down way, out of a proper cup with a hannle and all. Table-cloth as well, begad.'

Mrs. Dispin alwis done that sort o' thing well, mind. Twad'n out of no regards fer Alfy. But her's most mortle house-proud, and it comes natteral to her to have everything jus' so. To spaik the truth, her did'n consider Alfy worthy aw't, but her done it becus her mus' be the best housewife in the parish, and so's her cude throw it up to him that he'd got a better 'ome than he deserved.

So Jim stretched his legs in under the table, very plaised with hiszelf. 'I'll pack away this lot,' he said, 'and then I'll make mezel' comferable in the aisy cheer till Alfy comes home.'

He eat up everything that was aitable and then sot down to warm his toes. He expected Alfy wude be in any minute and he intended havin' a gude joke with 'n. However, he was so warm and comferable he valled right off to slape.

Bim-bye he waked up with a jump. The clock was strikin' zeb'm. He cude'n zee no signs of Alfy.

'My dear days,' he said, 'if the old dumman comes back I shall be ketched like a mouze in the braid-pan. Jim Davey, you'd better be loppin' along, quick.' So he flipped out the door, down droo the garden, and out over the hedge.

He need'n 'a-bin in sitch a tremenjis hurry, 'cus Mrs. Blissit had sevver'l nice bits o' scandal to tell up, so 'twas handier eight than zeb'm when Lucy Dispin got home. By that time the vire had all burned down low, and the durty platters was spraid all over the table.

She was furious, 'cus her reckoned her'd brought Alfy up differ'nt to that. He knowed very well he had to clear away all the things behind 'en when she was out the way, and wash 'em up clean and putt 'em away in their proper place. Furthermore, he shude have carr'd in a fresh log and putt on the vire.

Lucy putt her head out the door.

'Al-*fay!*'

No Answer.

'AL-FAY!'

'Alfy' looks a nice lovin' sort o'name in print, but you'd be surprised what Lucy Dispin cude make it sound like when her was in a bad timper. If there was a dog within harkening distance he'd jump out of his skin when Lucy gived a shout fer her ole man.

This time there wad'n no answer. The hens all started to zing, the owls flied out o' the trees, all the cats in the parish went home like graised lightnin'; but Alfy did'n appear.

Such thing had never happened bevore, and Mrs. Dispin was at a loss to know what to do next. Her thought of sevver'l things her'd do later on, but her cude'n start on none of 'em till Alfy arrived.

Now, accordin' to the way Alfy had got it all schemed out her nex' projec' should 'a-been to seek for 'n to the Rid Lion. And that's jis' what her was on the point o' doing, but zac'ly as her went to open the gaate who shude pass along the rawd but Jim Davey hiszelf. Mrs. Dispin said:

'Be you gwain to the pub, Mr. Davey? Well, there, that's a needless ques'ion. Anyway, if my man's in there, you plaise to tell 'n I'm home waitin' vor 'en, and I shall expec' to zee 'en within vive minutes.'

'I'll zee he gets the message if he'm there, missis. But I shude 'a-thought he'd hear you callin' jus' now. Tid'n much more 'n quarter of a mile.'

'I daun' want none o' your chick, Jim Davey. Nobody wude'n take the trouble to call fer you, that's a sure thing. They'd zooner zee 'ee gwain the oppozyte derection.'

"Twude be the most likely way you'd zee me trav'lin', missis. I'll make a bet Alfy wishes he'd alwis done the zame.'

'My husband have got a gude home, and the zooner he vinds his way to it the better 'twill be for 'en. And you jus' tell 'n zo.'

'I will, missis.'

Jim laafed as he walked on along the rawd. He said to hiszel', 'So I ab'm zee'd the end o' this yer caper, 'eet. Alfy not bin home! What's behind it all. I spause her thinks he've had his tay and gone again. Surely to goodness he ab'm broke her apern-strings arter all these years.'

Jim never wad'n the sort o' chap that makes plans. If he did he wude'n abide by 'em, mos' likely. But he was a turrable feller to do things on the spurt o' the moment. Jis' as he was passin' by Mrs. Webber's shop out comes Sarah Mundy. Cude'n 'a-bin a better person.

'Mrs. Mundy,' he says, 'have you yeard that Alfy Dispin have carted off Jinny Causey to the dance to Nackaburge, and left his awn wife behind! I can't believe it, can you?'

O' coorse, her had'n yeard no-such thing, but her wude'n admit it. Mrs. Mundy's one o' they that must alwis know everything.

'Cert'nly, I can believe it, Mr. Davey. Still waters rins deep, and is muddy to the bottom. I was'n gwain to mention it mezelf till I'd made sure, 'cus 'tis such a draidful thing fer poor Mrs. Dispin, and I don't like spraidin' tales o' that kind about. But tid'n the man's

119

fau't. That baggage of a Jinny Causey have been the ruination of more than one if the truth was told, and will be the ruination of Mr. Dispin, you mark my word.'

Jim considered he'd done all that was necessary to give the thing a start, so he said, 'Well, I'm vexed to yer it,' and went on with the zame. But Mrs. Mundy cude hardly reach as fur as Poll Starks's cottage without bustin'.

'Mrs. Sparks, what do you think? Alfy dispin have gone off to the dance to Nackaburge with Jinny Causey.'

Poll was so tooked aback that her went and gived herself away, bevore he had time to think.

'What! You don't say so, Mrs. Mundy?'

'Well, you can't say I wad'n the first to tell 'ee this time,' says Sarah; and Poll was proper wicked to think her had'n been more careful. However, her determined to make the best of a bad job, so as soon as Mrs. Mundy had gone off to break the news to a few more her putt on her hat quick, and away-do-go to Mrs. Dispin's cottage. Her found Lucy in a proper upset, but not quite the way her imagined.

'This is a draidful scat for you, Mrs. Dispin. I thought I mus' jus' rin along and tell 'ee how sorry I be vor 'ee; and if there's aught I can do——'

By this time Lucy Dispin had got back her breath.

'I don't zee what it have got to do with you, Poll Starks, anyway, and I'll thank you to mind yer awn affairs, if you can spare the time mindin' other people's.'

'Aw, of coorse, if you takes it like that, Mrs. Dispin, all well and gude, and I'm plaised to think your feelin's id'n hurted no more than they be. But if a husband of mine behaved like it I shude be glad of a little sympathy, that's all.

'What be you talking about? What have my husband done so speshul?'

'Mean to tell me you don't know, Mrs. Dispin? Why, he've rinned away with Jinny Causey.'

'What!'

'So Poll Starks sticked on a bit more to what Mrs. Mundy had told her and made up a very purty tale aw't.

'So that's it, is it?' says Lucy Dispin. 'He has the chick to come in yer and ait up the butiful tay I putt out for 'en, fit for a lord, and then goes gallivantin' off with that trollops. And I spause when he'm tired of her he'll come back yer to me. I shall be waitin' vor 'en, Mrs. Starks. If 'tis a day or a wik or a year, I shall be waitin' vor 'en, and I shall give 'n a welcome home which he won't ferget all the days of his life; not if he lives to be as old as Methusalum. But I shan't go the length of me nawse to look for 'en, Poll Starks, so you can take yerself and yer sympathy back where they come from. I ban't in need of either.'

So Alfy Dispin, out to the cross rawds, need'n 'a-bin 'feard of being discovered. He imagined scores o' volks out seekin' vor 'en with lanterns and dogs and all the rest aw't; but twad'n zo. His scheme had went wrong. But how was he to know that?

3.   AFTER THE DANCE

Poor Alfy sot down in the hedge and tried to think as well as he cude with his brains gwain round and round like a whirligig. He'd yeard bevore that when volks be wanderin' in the dark they'm ap' to go round in a circle. That's what he'd been and done; and now arter all that trouble and bother, and thinkin' he'd got miles away from home, yer he was only two minutes from his own door.

'Twas very discouragin', and Alfy cude 'a-cried almost. Tired as a dog, froze to the marrer, wet right droo to the skeen and bliddin' in a score places where he'd 'itched hiszelf in the brimmles or scat hiszelf agin hard things in the dark, he was a pitiful objic', sure nuff. He began to wish with all his 'art he'd never started on such a caper. It all looked so aisy when he planned it out, but nothin' had'n come to pass as he ordained for it to. He was in two minds about walkin' they vew yards and gwain back home.

But when he come to think it out, that wude'n do, neether.

'If I goes back now I shall be wiss off than ever, 'cus her'll want me to account for bein' away so long, and I don't zee what excuse I cude hatch up. 'Twude'n do to say I'd lost me memory and vound it again. None o' the volks on the paper done that. And if me memory come back all right, I shude'n gain no advantage from losting it. No; there's only one thing vor it. I mus' start off again. But this time I shan't do no climmin' over hedges and ditches. I shall stick to the rawd and chance it. 'Tid'n very

121

likely there'll be anybody about thees time o' night, and if I
hap'ms to rin into one o' the parties what be zeekin' vor me, I
shall lost me memory on the spot and let 'em get on with it.'

So Alfy turned his back once more on his home, and on the
lovin' wife who he imagined wude be jis' beginnin' to get anxious
about 'en, and he sot off to vind a place where he cude lost his
memory to. He travelled along the rawd towards Nackaburge.

When he first planned out his adventure he ordained bein'
discovered a lot furder away from home than Nackaburge. But
things had changed since then. Starvin' hungerd, shrammed to
death with the cold, and achin' in every limb he made up his
mind that Nackaburge was quite fur nuff away to answer his
purpose. That meant trapesin' another vive or zix mile, anyway,
and in the state he was now, it zeemed more like vive or zix
hunderd.

Fust-along he was feared of his life he wude meet with one o'
the parties out zeekin' vor 'en, and he kep' his eyes lookin' in all
derections, ready to hide away if he ketched zight of a lantern.
But arter a bit, when he'd got tireder and tireder he beginned to
wish he'd rin into zomebody purty quick and putt a end to his
misery. But there wad'n nobody to rin into, and his veet was like
two lumps o' laid. 'Twas as much as ever he cude do to drag wan
leg behind t'other.

'I shall go on till I gets to the outskirts o' the village,' he said to
hiszel', 'and then find zome place where I can lay down to and go
to sleep 'genst the mornin'. Then when I be discovered with me
memory all gone scat, 'twill look as if I've bin wanderin' about all
night. But I wish I'd got a bite o' zummat to stap the pangs in me
inzide. However, 'twill make it appear more real if I'm lookin'
half-starved, so p'r'aps 'tis all for the best.'

Alfy's sperrits rised up a bit, and he beginned to step it out
proper brisk. The rain had ceased for a bit, and he was able to get
a li'l warmth into his body. He even beginned to laaf again, when
he thought about the volks with lanterns straking about on the
moor, and the policeman riding into Barleycombe to report the
loss of Mr. Dispin; and the long account on the paper.

To-last he got handy to Nackaburge, and thought about
looking for zome place where he cude make hiszelf comferable
and rest for a nower or two. He did'n ordain sleeping very long,
cus he considered he ought to be zee'd wanderin' about very

early in the mornin', to give the volks the impression that he'd bin on the go all night. However, he wad'n to get to rest quite so quick as he thought. None of his plans did'n zeem to turn out right, zome'ow. I s'pause 'twas jidgment on 'en, for scheming out such falseness.

He'd jus' got oppozyte the lane that goes down past the Mill, and he thought down there very likely he'd vind the place he was lookin' vor, when he zee'd a vunny bright light up in the sky. He cude'n think what it cude be for a minute till he yeard the sound o' the horn and then he knowed 'twas a moter comin'. His first motive was to hide hiszel', but second thoughts, he decided to bide where he was to, and let the volks in the car zee 'en. He remembered one o' the cases on the paper where zome moter-car volks come vorward and said they'd zee'd such a body wanderin' on the rawd. Alfy thought 'twude be nice to have moter volks mixed up in it. They might be grand volks with hannles to their name, and would take interest in 'en when he was recoverin' from the shock. So he lopped on along the rawd where the moter must pass close to 'en.

But jis' as the car was gwain to ketch vore to 'en, Alfy yeard a hoss and trap comin' round the corner in the oppozyte derection. He zee'd they mus' meet right on the bend o' the rawd; and that's zac'ly what they done. The chap in the moter was gwain along a middlin' gude lick and when he suddenly come on the li'l speezin' lights o' the trap he blawed up his hooter to such extent he frightened Alfy out of ten years' growth.

But he frightened the hoss likewise. The glare o' the lights and the noise of the hooter made the poor baiste jump out of his harness purt' near. They did'n colliz ner nothin', and the feller in the moter did'n suspicion nothin' wrong, so he drived on. But the hoss give a couple more jumps, the near wheel o' the trap went right up over the hedge, and bevore a lamb cude have shook his tail the second time the driver was chucked out bang in the rawd.

Alfy jumped to the hoss's head, and led her back on the rawd; and then he went to see to the driver. To his surprise he vound 'twas a wumman. When he got to her, her was stood up and did'n zim none the wiss.

'Be you hurted, my dear?' says Alfy.

'My dear life,' her says; 'if that id'n Alfy Dispin. Well! Of all the wonders in the world!'

'Twas Jinny Causey!

Alfy was so tooked aback that he nearly gived hiszelf away. If he'd let out what was on the tip of his tongue he'd have upzet the whole applecart.

'Whatever brings you out yer this time o' night, Alfy?'

The ques'ion brought the li'l feller back to his sainses. He must remember what *had* brought'n out there, and act accordin'. He had'n meant to begin so soon, and he wished Jinny Causey to Halifax, cus her wad'n a bit the sort o' body he wanted to be vound by. However, he had to play his li'l game, else all his fuss and trouble wude be drowed away. Lucky for Alfy, Jinny went on talking, which give 'n more time to think.

'I've bin to the dance to Nackaburge,' her said. 'My cousin, Jim Causey, and his wife Bessie was to have went with me, but they was prevented the last minute so I was forced to drive alone. But what's fetched you all over yer? You ab'm bin to the dance fer certin. Your wife wude see about that.'

'Who might you be?' says Alfy, makin' his voice sound all weak and shaky.

'What do 'ee mean, who I be? Jinny Causey, I be. You ought to know my voice as well as I know yours, Alfy Dispin.'

'Why do you call me by that name?'

'What name shude I call 'ee by, fer gudeness saake? Ponshus Pilot or Charlie Chapman or what? Where be you gwain to?'

'I dunnaw.'

'Well, where have 'ee come from?'

'I dunnaw.'

Alfy was gettin' on fus' rate, he reckoned. All he wanted now was to get shut o' Jinny. P'raps 'twas just as well arter all. Her cude go back and report that her'd zee'd him wanderin' about like a man-a-lost. Then they'd all come zeekin' vor 'en; but he'd hide away till daylight, anyway.

Little did he draime that his wife was already thinkin' of him and Jinny in the zame breath.

'Gude night, young wumman,' he said, in a holler sort o' voice, and started on the rawd.

'Yer, not so vast,' says Jinny, ketchin' him hold by the arm. 'That's not your way.'

''Tis the way I mus' go,' he says, like a man in a draime.

'Aw, is it? Well, if you ban't fit to look arter yerzel', you mus' be looked arter, that's all. You get up in my trap, and I'll drive 'ee home.'

124

This did'n suit Alfy's book.

'I've got a long journey to go, and mus' be movin',' he says. But her held on to 'en.

'You've got a long journey all right, but not that derection. Up you get, and not talk so much.'

This was gettin' sayrious, and Alfy did'n know his words, quite. None o' the cases he'd read about went like this. He made another effort to move on, but Jinny had tight hold.

'Now,' her says, 'be you gwain to get up or must I haive 'ee up?'

Alfy's only a li'l bit of a chap and Jinny's a hefty gurt maid, strong as a young hoss. He struggled hard to get away, but 'twas like a rabbut tryin' to get out of a gin. Her was jis' gwain to try to lift 'n up in trap when a man come along ridin' hoss-back.

'Twas young Fred Ozegude. He'd bin to the zame dance as what Jinny had, and he was now homeward. All-to-once he zee'd what he took to be a man and a wumman vightin' in the rawd. He gived a shout and jumped off his hoss.

'That you, Fred?'

'Bless my zaul, 'tis Jinny Causey. What's matter, Jinny?'

'Nothin' the matter, only I've jis' come across Alfy Dispin. Zomebody's given him too much to drink, and now he does'n know whether he's gwain or coming back. What a wicked shame to give drink to a waik-minded poor mortle like him. Help me lif' 'en up in trap, and I'll take'n back to his wife.'

'Best thing to do with 'n. He'll get rinned over if us leaves 'n out in rawd.'

Alfy fought like a taygur, but he had'n got a ghost of a chance with they two.

'Properly mad with drink, he is,' says Fred. ''Tid'n safe fer you to have 'n up in trap with 'ee without us binds 'n up. Have 'ee got anything suitable?'

Jinny found a buckle-strap in the trap, so they putt that one around Alfy's two veet, and then Fred tied his two hand-wristis behind his back with his hankcher. Then they lied poor li'l Alfy on the bottom o' the trap like a trussed fowl. Jinny drived the trap and Fred rode along behind till they come to the head o' the village, where he had to turn off.

'Think you'll be all right, now, Jinny, or shall I come on with 'ee?'

'No. You get on 'ome, Fred. I shall be all right.'

So Fred Ozegude left 'em, and Jinny drived on to Alfy's cottage. What his veelin's was like you must think out fer yerzel'. I cude'n tell 'ee, fer certin.

Mrs. Dispin was gone to bed, so Jinny drowed up a han'ful o' li'l stones to the winder. Purt' near frightened the life out o' the wumman. Her wad'n too swit-tempered by half when her went to bed, so it did'n improve matters very much. Her got out o' bade and poked her head out o' winder.

'Who's there?'

"Tis Jinny Causey. I've got your husband yer, drunk as a lord.'

4.   ALFY COMES HOME

Of all the people in the world that shude have met with Mrs. Dispin in the mood her was then, Jinny Causey was the very last. For howers on end Lucy had bin turning over in her mind all the most draidful things her cude do to this-yer maid. Her was determined fer one thing to have her up bevore the jidge. Her wad'n quite sure whether 'twas bigamy or braich o' promish, but her was gwain to vind out the very nex' day, if her had to pay a turney to tell her.

'I reckon her can be putt away to prisin fer cartin' off another wumman's husband like that. And if her id'n sent to prisin 'twill be such exposure vor her, her won't be able to show her faace again in the parish fer a gudish bit.'

That was what Lucy Dispin had bin thinking to herzel', and a lot more o' the zame zort. So you can jist imagine, when Jinny Causey come wakin' her up in the middle o' the night, and had the chick to zay her'd brought back her husband, as cool as if her was returnin' a pair of bellises which her'd borreed, there was murder in Mrs. Dispin's 'art.

O' coorse, Jinny was quite innocent of what the other wumman was thinkin' about her. She reckoned she was doin' a kindness to the both of 'em, and natcher'ly expected Alfy's wife wude be thankful to her fer taking him home instaid o' leaving him to be rinned over. So when Mrs. Dispin banged down the winder fit to break every pane o' glass, her did'n pay no 'tention to it, 'cus her thought the wumman was putt out with her husband fer gwain away and gettin' drunk like it. Jinny got down from her sate, thinkin

Mrs. Dispin wude require assistance to get her ole man out from the trap. Her was middlin surprised, I can tell 'ee, when the other wumman started gwain for her as if her wude tear her limb from limb.

'You brass-facid huzzey! How dare you come and show yourzel' like this? And where have you bin to, I shude like to know.'

'Never you mind about me, Mrs. Dispin. You zee to your husband. That'll take all your spare time, without nosing into my business. So you please to mind yer awn.'

'I shude think '*tis* my business,' says Lucy in that voice of hers. 'And all the world shall yer of it.'

'They must be middlin' deave if they can't. Be you gwain to take your husband out o' my trap or no? I wish I had'n took the trouble to bring 'en back to 'ee.'

'I wonder you had, I'm sure. After you'd took the trouble to 'tice him away, 'twas better-fit you kep' 'n away, altogether.'

'What do you mean by 'tice 'en away?' says Jinny. 'If I wanted to take anybody away 'twude be zomebody differ'nt to he. Things like that is only took by women what can't get nothing better.'

Then there was a middlin' fine shindy, you mid be sure; and Alfy forced to lie there in the bottom o' the trap and harken to it all. He larned a lot o' things about hiszel' which he never knowed bevore; but nothin' to his credit.

Poor feller! What a differ'nce to what he ordained. He'd picshered hiszelf bein' tooked home in zome grand body's carriage, with a docter sot bezide 'n feeling his pulses, and everybody takin' the utmost care of 'en and walkin' about the place on tippy-toes so's he shude'n be disturbed; and him tucked up in bed with the best of everything to ait and drink so's to bring back his strength and zee if his memory wude return or no. Volks wude keep callin' to his houze to know how he was gettin' on, and up to the Rid Lion all the talk wude be about Alfy Dispin and his lost memory. Into Barleycombe market they volks what was acquainted with 'en wude boast about it to they what wad'n. And bim-bye, when he got strong enough jis' to potter about (but not do no work, which wude be bad for 'en) people wude point him out to one-tother:

'Look, there's Mr. Dispin, the gen'lman what have lost his memory. He can't remember nothin' what happened bevore such-an'-such a time.'

That's how Alfy had imagined it, and now look at it. No parties
out zeekin' vor 'en; no more notice took of his gwain than if he'd
went out in garden to cut a cabbage. His missis gone to bed as
usual, without botherin' her head where he was to; no policeman
brought acquainted with it; no nothing. And him brought home
like a calf bein' took to market. The whole thing was all wrong,
and he cude'n think what to be up to next. The only thing he was
clear about was that he must lost his memory now, completely.
But what he cude'n understand was why his missis was bully-
raggin' Jinny Causey fer taking him away. O' coorse, he did'n
know nothin' about the li'l ball which Jim Davey had started
rollin', and he cude'n zee fer the life of him what Jinny had got to
do wai' 't. Nor yet Jinny cude'n, neether, and to-last her said to
Lucy:

'Look yer, Mrs. Dispin, I dunnaw what you mean by me taking
your husband away, but if you says it again I shall slap your faace.
And I shall slap 'n hard.'

Lucy knowed her cude do it, so her let it go to that.

'Now, be you gwain to take your husband out o' my trap or no,
'cus I want to be gettin' home.'

'They what putt 'n in shude take 'n out.'

'That's very soon done,' says Jinny. With the zame, her let
down the back o' the trap, ketched Alfy hold by the two veet, and
bevore he cude do aught to succour hiszelf he was haaled out and
went down bump, like a bag o' meal. Then Jinny tooked her
buckle strap off his veet and Fred Ozegude's hankcher, and
away-do-go.

Alfy was able to stan' up, now. His wife said to 'en:

'Now, you, jis' you come in-houze and give account o' yerzel'.'

So Alfy said his little piece.

'I've got a long way to go and mus' be on my journey. I'll wish
you gude night.'

'Aw, will 'ee?' her saith. 'You'll wish ever so many things
bevore I've done with 'ee.' Her ketch 'n hold by one yer and
walked 'n indoors. Alfy did'n show fight 'cus he was suppaused to
be very ill and weak.

Lucy tried every way her cude to get sainse out of 'en, but all
he'd zay was that he had a long ways to go and must be on the
rawd. Her had all the works o' the world to keep 'n from gwain
out the door. Her tried to make 'n go to bed, but he wude'n go

128

up over the stairs. He made wise 'twas all strange to 'en. So to-last her said:

'Aw, wull, you can jis' sit down there till you gets sober. I'm gwain up over. You won't hurt, fer certin, after they two aigs and all the 'am you had fer tay. I'll go along and you can volley when you mind to.'

Her turned the kay in the lock, took 'n with her and went off to bade.

Alfy sot down with his inzide cryin' out fer zummat to ait. But what was it her said about his tay? Aigs an' 'am? He had'n had no aigs an' 'am, ner nothin' else since the middle o' the day bevore. More'n twelve howers since he'd had a bite of any sort; and her telling about the lovely tay he'd had.

The very thought aw't made 'n ten times wiss. 'Am, by jo! What he wude give fer a slishe now, between two hunks o' braid. His teeth went all cold and wet at the very idaya.

Lucy distinc'ly said he had his tay. Cude it be a fac' that he railly had lost his memory? No. Nobody's inzide cude veel like his if it had two aigs in it. Not even if it had one aig, never mind about the 'am. He'd never bin so starvin' hungerd in all his life.

'Twude'n 'a-bin so bad if he'd bin out bezide a hay-rick or in under the hedge where he knowed there wad'n nothin' to be had. But now he was within a vew veet of plenty. Out o' one door, along a little drangways and in the cubberd. If her putt out 'am fer tay, as her said, there must be more where that come from.

Alfy tried hard to go to slape and ferget his misery. But 'twas no gude. The gnawin' pain in his innerds kep' 'n awake. Then he thought to hiszel':

'If I was to slishe off a li'l bit very careful, her'd never notice 'twas gone. That wude stay me over 'genst the mornin'. Her's vast aslape now, fer certin.'

He tooked off his butes and creeped out as quiet as a mouze, with a lighted cannle. Ees, there was the 'am right nuff. A thumpin' gurt piece. 'Her'll never miss a slishe off o' that,' he thought. 'I'll bide yer and ait it, and take care not to leave no crumbs about.'

Alfy tooked out his pocket-knive and knacked off a bit of 'am, and a hunch o' braid. It brought tears to his eyes as it went down. But 'twas only sufficient to make 'n railise how hungerd he was. 'A teeny bit more won't notice.' So he another go to it. A comferable feelin' beginned to go down his inzide, the fust for howers.

"Twude be nice to injoy the last bit bevore the vire,' he thought. 'I'll be careful not to drap no crumbs about.'

So he hat off one more bit, a trifle thicker thees time, fer he was gettin' reckless, and carr'd it back to his sate bevore the vire. Then he railised he was dry. Turrable dry, he was. Dry, fit to chuck. The salty 'am had made it wiss. Come what wude, he must have a drink.

Alfy knowed perfec'ly well there was a bottle o' beer in the box bezide the pump-traw, out in back-'ouze. Lucy made it a rule to have a bottle or two there, covered up with a bag. Her reckoned they kep' better where 'twas cold. The thoughts of a bottle o' beer was more than Alfy cude indure. If he drinked one now he cude manage to replace it zome'ow to-morra, bevore his missis discovered the gwain aw't. He went along, as soft as he cude, out droo the back kitchen. The nex' door was barred on the inzide, and he had a bit o' trouble to make'n slide back quiet. 'Twas a trifle stiff, and he held his breath all he cude, but he had to make a bit o' noise. 'Twas only very little, however, and he reckoned his missis wude be snorin' butiful by thees time.

That was another of Alfy's li'l mistakes.

He vound the bottles where he expected. But 'tis a difficult job to lift one bottle out without makin' a sound. He jis' chinked it up agin the nex' one; but 'twas nothing to mention, and Alfy went back to the kitchen smilin' to hiszel' at the thoughts of the lovely time he was gwain to have.

His smile died right away when he zee'd his wife stood in the middle o' the floor. He had one try to hide the bottle away in under his weskit. But 'twas a poor attemp'. Bezides, there was the 'am and brain on the corner o' the table.

Lucy lookid at 'en fer a minute or two, and Alfy's teeth rattled more'n ever they did with the cold.

'I'm pleased to zee your memory's come back all right,' her saith. 'If you can remember the way to the beer you can remember the way to bed. Have a try and zee what you can do towards it.'

Alfy started in a shaky voice about havin' a long journey to go. But Lucy cheemed in:

'Shall 'ee try by yourself, or will I take the rollin'-pin and help 'ee?'

Alfy tried by hiszelf.

And now his memory is better than ever 'twas. There's some things he'd give anythin' to ferget: but he can't. Lucy won't let 'en to.

JUDGMENT

Nathaniel Webber's a masterpiece. He *is* the most bigative body ever I come across, man or wumman; and that's saying zummat if you include the both.

Nathaniel's turrable sankeymonious local praicher and all the rest aw't. Mind, I ban't sayin' a word agin that. There's nothin' I likes better mezel', than to harken to a gude praicher. But I reckon Nath carr's it a bit too fur. There's no rhyme or raison with 'n. Accordin' to his estimation, everybody's wrong with exception of him. Tom Zalter used to zay Nath wude have a turrable lonely time when he got to heaven, 'cus he'd have the place all to hiszel'. Nath reckons everybody is wicked if they do's ort differ'nt to what their vather and gran'vather done bevore 'em. So he considers all new inventions is the work of Ole Nick.

You'd 'a-thought he'd have got used to the ole wireless by now, when 'tis in half the houses in the parish. But not he. I'll tell 'ee what he said to me about it, and then you can zee for yerzelf.

Las' wik us had a turrable storm and Nathaniel's houze was strick with the lightnin'. Scat the chumley-pot clane off into the garden. Thinder-bolt they reckoned 'twas, although they never found no trace of such thing arterwards. Mrs. Webber declared her zee'd it with her awn eyes.

'Like a ball o' vire,' her said. 'Come straight down from the sky, he did, jis' like as if he'd bin shat out from a gun, and he hat off the chumley-pot as clane as a wissle and scat 'n abroad into tain-thousand pieces. Where he went to arter that I can't think, but I reckon us would vind 'n buried in the ground if us was to dig right plaace.'

There's some volks about what will tell 'ee that Mrs. Webber never zee'd no sitch thing. Lizzie Zalter fer one.

131

'I've been along o' Mrs. Webber more'n once when there's been thinder about,' said Mrs. Zalter, 'and the fus' thing her always do's is to rin up over stairs and stick her haid in under the bed-clothes. And there her bides till 'tis all over, and nothin' won't shift her. So how her cude zee a thinder-bolt I can't think, unless her valled asleep and draimed about it.'

However, Nathaniel reckons he knaws what caused it.

"Tis on account o' so much o' this-yer ole wireless, Jan Stewer,' he said to me. 'That's the whole and sole raison fer 't.'

'Do 'ee think zo, Nath?'

'I don't think nothin' about it. I'm sure aw't. 'Tis a jidgment on the land by raison of the wickedness o' the people.'

'How do 'ee make out 'tis wickedness?' I said.

'Wickedness? Of coorse 'tis wickedness. What can 'ee term it else? Was it ever intended to be? Was it ever ordained that us shude harken to volks telling a hunderd mile away? Us was given yers to yer with, wad'n us? That's what it saith in the Gude Buke, daun' it? "He that hath yers to yer, lat 'n yer," it says. It daun' zay, "He that id'n satisfied with the yers that was give to 'en shall putt a contraption on his head and harken to what's gwain on hunderds o' miles away." Do it zay that? Did ever you rade that it said that?'

'I dunnaw that ever I did, Nath.'

'No, and you never won't, and therefore 'tis gwain contry to what providence ordained, and there's bound to come a jidgment vor it.'

'But neether it don't zay, "He what id'n satisfied with the eyes what was give to 'en shall putt on a pair o' sparticles." But I've zee'd you putt on sparticles, scores o' times.'

'You'm spaiking vanity, Jan Stewer. Nort but vanity. I putts on sparticles becus me natteral eyes is waik, and arter I've got 'em on I can only zee such things as 'twas ordained vor me to zee. I can't zee what's gwain on in the nex' county. But your yers id'n waik. You can yer all that's gude fer 'ee to yer; and a bit more zometimes, I don't doubt. And fer you to putt thikky-there ole halter on yer haid and zay you can yer the volks talkin' up to Lunnon only comes of a proud look and a high stummick. Whether you railly can yer all the things you says you can, or whether you can't id'n vor me to jidge, but if you can't then 'tis tain times wiss, 'cus 'tis only falsity 'pon top of rebelliousness.'

'Wull, Nath,' I said, 'so fur as that's consarned, it don't zay that volks shude ride about in moters, or go up in airyplanes, and scores of other things bezides. You mid all-so-well condemn the whole lot.'

'And zo I do condemn it, Jan Stewer. Een saison and out o' saison. I've condemned it into the pole-pit to chapel. I've condemned it from the strate corners and the houze-tops, mornin', noon and night; and I've condemned they what takes part in it. 'Tis all part and parcel o' the zame thing. 'Tis all sinful luss o' the flesh, and 'tis no wonder there's thinder-bolts.'

'You goes too fur, Nath.'

'That's where you makes mistake to, Jan Stewer. I don't go too fur. I don't go at all. I bides where I was putt to. 'Tis the rest of 'ee what goes too fur, and if you ban't very careful you'll fall out over the edge, and there won't be none to ketch 'ee hold and putt 'ee back again, and you'll have nort but wailing and gashing yer teeth. Volks be settin' theirzels up agin providence with their flippin' about the face of the earth, and their flappin' up to the sky and their floppin' down bottom o' the say. Flip, flap, flop, that's all they thinks about. Us ban't burds and us ban't veesh, and fer we to try to mimic such things is idolatry and transgression, and you can't call it no other. And then you all comes along with this tale about wireless. That's a lie to start wai'. What have you got sticked up there?'

He pointed to my air-oil.

'How can you term it wireless when you've got a long length o' wire up in the air fer everybody to see? You might jis'-so-well zay your face is hairless when you've got wiskers all the way around. I tell 'ee 'tis all wrong.'

'What is, Nath, my wiskers?'

'I don't mean to zay your wiskers is wrong, I mean the way volks is carr'ing on. Us must expect to have judgment vor it. It have happened zo bevore and 'twill hap'm zo again. You've raid about the tain plagues of Aigyp', ab'm 'ee? But you daun' need to go back so fur as that. You've zee'd it hap'm bevore yer awn eyes.'

'I dunnaw that I have, Nath.'

'Yas, you have. You knows very well you have, only you'm like the rest o' the sons o' Belial, you closes yer eyes to the warnin' and hardens yer 'art. What about Farmer Burridge's black 'oss?'

'What about 'n, Nath?'

'Wad'n it proved that Ned Burridge barginned for thik 'oss with Wi'yum Lake of a Zindy? And gwain 'ome from church, of all plaaces! Vifty pound he agreed to pay 'en, and *did* pay it. Whether he acsh'ly handed over the money of a Zindy I can't zay; but that daun' make no odds. Be that as it may, he took the 'oss 'ome on the Mondy and on the Chewsdy mornin' he went out and found 'en in the ditch with his leg broke, so's he had to be shat. What else do 'ee call that but a jidgment?'

'But what about Wi'yum Lake? He had the vifty pound. Did'n he ought to be shat, too, daun' 'ee think?'

'You can depend on one thing, Jan Stewer; the money won't do 'en no gude.'

'I don't say 'twas right thing vor 'em to do business on a Zindy, Nath,' I said. 'I ban't upholdin' that fer one instant. There's a-plenty other days fer that. But I wude'n zay that was why the 'oss broke his leg, 'cus I had a 'oss once what broke his leg, and I did'n bargin for 'en of a Zindy.'

'Very likely not. But I'll venter to zay you done zummat else you did'n ought to.'

'I derzay I did,' I said.

'I'll warrant you did. And then again look at Seth Passmore's wive. What happened to she? Chaited her awn sister out o' tain pound, her did. When poor ole man Zellick died, her vather that was, and all his sticks was putt up to oction, her wrote and told her sister they fetched twenty pound less than what they did, and her hanged on to the differ'nce. And what happened to she?'

'Her valled down daid.'

'That's right.'

'Hold hard a minute, Nath. The very zame thing happened to Mrs. Tapper up to Ratver Coort. Her valled along daid, too. And what have you got to say agin she?'

'I dunnaw that I wants to zay ort agin Mrs. Tapper.'

'No, and you cude'n if you was to try, although you'm expert at it. Her done more gude in one wik than you and me putt together have ever done in tain years.'

'I wude'n zay that,' says Nath.

'Aw, wude'n 'ee? I wude, then. You start and tell whatever gude you've done fer anybody, and then I'll tell 'ee a vew things Mrs. Tapper done, and us'll zee who'll win.'

'You'm like all the rest o' the haythen,' says Nath. 'You tries to get out aw't by making excuses. But excuses won't do 'ee no gude. I tell 'ee this-yer ole wireless is like a gude many things else, now-a-days. 'Tis flyin' in the face o' providence, and the cause of half the trouble in the country.'

'But 'twas your houze was strick, not mine. I shude 'a-thought it shude be t'other way around.'

'That's jis' where 'tis to,' he saith. 'The just has got to suffer fer the unjust.'

'Half a minute, Nath,' I said. 'I can't remember raiding anywhere that us be suppaused to keep a cask o' cider in the cubberd in under the stairs.'

'There's gude raison fer that, Jan Stewer. Do you think the Almighty don't know what turrable bad drinking watter 'tis to my place?'

FOR THE GOOD OF THE CAUSE

1. BAL MASQUE

I'm seekin' for a Cause. I wants one of me own, to keep handy in case o' need. I've come to conclusion that a Cause wude be a very useful thing to have about. You don't hap'm to have one you cude spare me, I suppause. I wude'n mind payin' vor't, if 'twas suitable. But it mus' be a Gude Cause.

I reckon if you've got a Gude Cause you can avoid sufferin' a lot of bother and trouble from other volks, 'cus you can make yerzell such a nuisance they'll be 'feared to come near 'ee. Furthermore, you can protect yerzell agin all the other people what has got Gude Causes. Or if you owes anybody a gridge you can make their lives a proper misery. You can go tormentin' 'em all howers o' the day and night, hinedering 'em in their work, or makin' 'em do all manner o' stoobid things till they hates the very zight of 'ee. All you've got to zay is, "Tis fer the Gude of the Cause.' Whichever of 'ee says that fust is the winner.

Drec'ly anybody says, "Tis fer the Gude o' the Cause,' you mus' be ready to putt up with no end of uncomferableness and ill-convenience, and be prepared to make yerzell look a bigger fule than what you do ordnery times.

And you muzzen zay, 'Hang the Cause,' or 'Darn the Cause,' or whatever's on the tip o' yer tongue. Ner you muzzen wish the Cause to the fust place you thinks of; not even to Halifax. If you do, people will think you'm a dreadful wicked body, and they'll zay wiss things about 'ee than if you took too much to drink, or putt a stick about your wive.

Zome volks makes a 'obby of Causes. Like ole Mother Row over to Week St. Agnes. Her've got Causes in galore. If you zees ole Mother Row comin' in the front gaate you can depend upon it her's bringing along a Cause of zome zort.

Of coorse, us daun' call her ole Mother Row to her faace, cus her's very much the vine lady, or thinks she is. But behind her back that's the very laiste o' the names zome people has got for her. When Mrs. Row says, "Tis all fer the Gude of the Cause,' you'm suppaused to be finished. You muzzen zay a word for yerzell arter that, or else you'm one o' the lost sheep. It daun' make no odds how bad 'tis vor you so-long as 'tis gude vor the Cause.

But p'r'aps you dunnaw what a Cause is. Well, I'll tell 'ee. The Cottage 'Ospital, that's a Cause, and the Distric' Nurse is a Cause, and the Women's Sociable Union is a Cause; cause of more strife and bad-frien'ship in this parish than all the rest putt together. Church Expenses is a Cause once a year, and so's Chapel Anniversary, and the Bell-ringers is a Cause when they'm jue to have a outin'. All the rest o' the year they'm only a cause of annoyance.

When they can't vind a Cause in their awn parish they invents a fancy one, like Haythen Missionaries, or the Home for Bline Mice. And then zomebody what wude'n take a scrap o' notice of 'ee ordnery times comes and makes a fuss of 'ee and persuades 'ee to do zummat fulish vor the Gude o' the Cause.

So when I zee'd Mrs. Row approachin' the door, I said to my Ann, 'Ullaw, another Gude Cause.' And Ann said, 'Must be. Her wude'n call yer, else.'

O' coorse, us daun' care nort about Mrs. Row, 'cus her id'n nothin' to we. Her daun' belong to the parish, and her never comes to our houze without her wants to get zummat. Her've alwis got her vinger in zome ole pie, eetherways a jumbo-sale or a bazaar, and then her'll come beggin' fer old 'ats, or garments, or a bit o' butter or craime, or a caake. And my Ann is never back'erds in comin' vorrad at sitch times. Her'll never zend 'em away without zummat.

But 'twas a differnt matter this time. The Cause was the Distric' Nurse, which is a very gude cause, and one us alwis suscribes to. But Mrs. Row wad'n beggin' fer money. Her rattled off a long ole rigmarole about a balmasky over to Barleycombe. Her keeped on about this-yer balmasky. Us did'n knaw a bit what 'twas, and us did'n trouble to ax, 'cus us daun' like Mrs. Row and that's all there is to it. Spesh'ly my wive. Her can't abear the wumman, 'cus her putts on sich airs. The only thing us cude gather was, that

137

us was expected to dress up in zome fancy togs and go to this-yer kickshaw. That finished mother, and her said, 'No.'

I was for wrappin' it up a bit more tidy like, in a manner o' spaikin'. I said 'twas very nice of her to take the trouble to come and ax me, and I shude have liked to take part if I cude, and I hoped 'twude be a success, but 'twad'n nothin' in my line, and zo on and zo vorth. But mother did'n go to all that trouble. Her said, 'No, mam, thank you. I shude'n think o' doin' such a thing.'

And that was the end o' that; or us thought 'twas. But us ought to 'a-knawed better. You can't get rid of a Gude Cause as aisy as that is.

'Twad'n but the very nex' day us had the shock of our life. Who shude I zee comin' in the gaate but Squire Porter and his gude lady, and Mrs. Jinkins, the docter's wive. You cude have knacked me down with a straw-mot when I zee'd that lot troopin' up the path.

It zo happened that mother had that minute been upstairs and clained herzell, so her was lookin' her best, as you mid zay. Lucky thing vor they, that was, 'cus her was in a zight better mood than what her wude 'a-bin if they'd ketched her all untidy. Makes a tremenjis differ'nce to a wumman how her's lookin' when there's other females about.

I'm bothered if this lot had'n come on the zame arrant as Mrs. Row, only they did'n know her'd been the day bevore. And they started all dree to-once. What one cude'n think of tother cude. O' coorse, us cude'n tick they off the zame as us did Mrs. Row. Us had to let they get on with their yappin'. And you knows how 'tis with people like that; you can't putt 'em off very aisy, 'cus they've got answer ready fer every objection you putt vorrad. And 'tid'n like as if they was people us don't like. The Squire and Mrs. Porter is two o' the very best, and anybody in the parish wude do any mortle thing to plaise Mrs. Jinkins, 'cus her'd do anything her cude vor they.

Mrs. Porter started the ball rollin'.

'You zee, Mrs. Stewer,' her said, 'this is vor the Distric' Nurse, so 'tis for every parish to take their share. Us dree have bin appointed committee for Muddlecombe, and as you know, Muddlecombe alwis reckons to be up-zides with other plaaces in such matters, and a bit a-haid if possible. Every year us has to get up to zummin to raise money, but this time us be gwain to try a new idaya.'

'A balmasky, I believe,' says my Ann, as cule as you like. Her'd remembered the word from yesterdy. If anybody had offered me vive pound I cude'n have repaited it. The gen'lvolks opened their eyes, too.

'You knows about it, then?' says Mrs. Jinkins. I cude zee her was proper tooked back to think my missis cude use such a word. Ann was proud of herzel', too.

'I'd yeard that's what 'twas gwain to be,' her says, as if her was accustomed to have balmaskys with every meal.

'That's splendid,' says Squire. 'They've stuck me in cheerman, so I'm anxious Muddlecombe shude come up to scratch, and I said drec'ly, "We must have Mr. and Mrs. Stewer."'

'What is it to do, zur?' I said.

'Well, 'tis a ball, Jan.'

'What do 'ee mean, a dance?'

'That's right, a dance,' he says; and my Ann cheemed in, 'Of coorse 'tis a dance. What did you think 'twas?'

I cude have said, 'The zame as you,' but I did'n think 'twas worth-a-while. But her had no more idaya what 'twas than I had, not till squire spoke.

'Why do 'em call it balmasky?' I axed.

'Aw,' says Mrs. Jinkins, 'that's what the French terms it.'

'Did'n you know that was French?' says Ann.

'No,' I thought to mezell, 'nor you neether, not bevore now.' But I did'n give the ole dear away, 'cus I thought one fule in the vamily was quite 'nuff. 'Is it jist a ordnery dance?' I said; 'cus zomehow it did'n zeem to fit in with all Mrs. Row's palarver.

'It is and it id'n,' says Mrs. Jinkins. 'You zee, balmasky railly means a mask ball.'

'The zame thing,' says Ann.

"Tis, so fur as I'm consarned,' I said. 'But what can you do wai't when you've got it.?'

Squire laafed. 'You'm like me, Jan,' he says, 'not very well acquainted with things o' this kind. But I'll tell 'ee what 'tis to do.'

So then he explained it, and from what I cude make out, 'twas a ordinary dance so fur as kickin' yer heels about, but everybody wears a black mask over their eyes, so's other volks shan't know who they be, and they trigs theirzells out in all manner o' fanciful togs to look like kings and quanes and fairies and black men or whatever they fancies.

'Like the Vith o' November,' I said.

'Aw, differ'nt to that,' says Mrs. Porter, "cus you only gets the nice people to dress up vor a mask ball.'

What's think o' that? You can't larn they sort o' people nothin'. They'm up to all the tricks imaginable. I cude zee my Ann sit up and take notice when her said that. 'Twas beginnin' to get dangerous.

'You'd better putt me down for fairy, yer 'onner,' I said. 'That wude be about suitin' me, I reckon.'

'I was jis' thinkin', my dear,' says Squire to Mrs. Porter, 'Jan cude go very well in they clothes of 'Enry Eight us have got home.'

'The very identical,' her says. "Enry Eight's wiskers was very similar to Mr. Stewer's so they'd fit in nice. You'd look fus'-rate in it, Mr. Stewer, and 'tis a butiful costume.'

"Tis very kind of 'ee, mam,' I said, 'and I'm much obliged fer the offer, but I'd sooner you let zomebody have it that was more suitin' to it. Now, there's Mr. Cann. His proper name is 'Enry, so 'twude be jis' right.'

'The name don't make no odds,' says Mrs. Porter. 'Of coorse, Mr. and Mrs. Cann are very nice and all that, but they'd hardly be the ones to appreciate a mask ball. I don't expec' 'twude be in their line.'

'No, I don't reckon it wude,' says Ann. I cude zee it was one more stap on the downward path.

'Of coorse,' says Mrs. Jinkins,' "Enry Eight was fat.'

'Yas, you zee mam,' I said, 'he was very fat and I be theen as a herrin'.'

'How do you know how fat he was?' says Ann. 'Twas on the tip o' me tongue to zay I'd zee'd the feller scores o' times, but I thought possibly they'd know 'twas lies, so I said, 'Mrs. Jinkins jis' said so.'

'Yas, he was rather fat,' says Mrs. Porter, 'but that don't make very much odds. You cude aisy make yerzell look fat with a cushion or two. You cude wad you husband out with a cushion, cude'n 'ee, Mrs. Stewer?'

'Certainly, I cude,' her says, only to glad to make it more ockerd vor me than what it wude be else. 'Or if I knowed jis' where he had to be fat to I cude putt a bolster around 'en.'

'I don't think I shude like it,' I said. 'Everybody wude know it wad'n natteral in that short space o' time.'

'Nobody wude'n know 'ee at all,' says Mrs. Jinkins. 'That's the buty of it. Anybody can go in whatever costume they likes and nobody can't own 'em with they maskis on their faces.'

'Twas the biggest paacel o' nonsainse ever I came across, but you can't very well say that to they sort o' people. I tried every way I cude think o' to turn 'em off from it, but the more objections I putt vore the more they yapped to make their awn tale gude.

'I shude'n know how to look like 'Enry Eight,' I said, 'and fer certain I shude'n know what to zay.'

'You ab'm got to zay a word,' says Mrs. Porter, 'and you'm bound to look right 'cus the clothes makes 'ee do that. And us have got everything, crown and all.'

'Crown?' I said. 'What was the feller, then?'

'Why,' says Squire, 'he was King. You've yeard of King 'Enry Eight, surely, the chap what had zix wives.'

'Did he, begad,' I says. 'Do you pervide wives and all?'

'If you like,' says Squire.

'Then you can strike me out. I've got more than I can do to putt up with one. Vive more and I shude require a harp as well as a crown.'

'Well, that's Jan settled, anyway,' says the Squire. 'Now what about Mrs. Stewer?'

'Don't bother about me,' her says. 'I shall have all my work cut out to see to him.'

'No you daun't,' I says. 'Both or neether, and neether for choice.'

'That lovely dress of Ann Bowling,' says Mrs. Porter to Squire. 'She'd look a rale quane in that one.'

'Who was Ann Bowling?' says mother.

'Wive of 'Enry Eight,' her says. 'Zo 'tis zac'ly right. The dress wude fit you very nice, and there waun' be a hansomer one in the rume, fer certin.'

That done it. Drec'ly they said mother shude wear a lovely dress and look like a quane I knowed my last hope was gone.

Zo I had to be trigged up like a merry-ander, and be 'Enry Eight, with a bolster fer a stommick. Thanks be it wad'n 'Enry Ninth, else p'r'aps I shude want a feather bed.

2.   KING FOR A NIGHT

I've no desire to be a king, I can tell 'ee that much. Anybody can have their job for me, that's if they'm all like 'Enry Eight. I had it for one night, and that will last me a lifetime. If I had to look vorrad to that every day o' me life I shude drown mezell, and that's tellin' of 'ee straight.

They tell about 'appy as a king; but if that's anybody's idaya of 'appiness, walkin' about like a fancy lamp-shade, afraid to zit down 'feared what might hap'm, covered all over with spangles like a sailor's pin-cushion, and tettyvated up with ribbins like the fus' prize and champion in a cart-'oss parade, they can have it. I daun' want it.

Feller might jis-so-well be a Punch an' Judy shaw and have done wai' t. No, I wude'n have that job not if they offered me a pound a wik and me keep. Fus' chance I got I shude off with the lot of it, slip on me burches and leggins, and flip out the back door; and they'd have to go a long way to find me, too.

I spause 'tis better now-a-days. Kings had got more sainse than to go about decorated up like a Lord Mayor's Show. And they've got other business to attend to bezides struttin' around like a stag turkey.

But Squire assured me that they things I had on was zacly zame as what 'Enry Eight used to wear. All I can zay is, if he had to go droo all that fuss and bother every day to get dressed and putt up with zix wives into the bargin, then 'tis no wonder he was a bit crotchety zometimes, as they zay he was.

Squire sent along all the togs in a gurt baskit, by young Dickey Ozegude. 'Bout o' leb'm o'clock in the mornin' that was, and us had'n got to start from home bevore zeb'm, so us had nice time to do it in.

My hyvers! I was properly frightened when us opened the lid o' the baskit and tooked out they things one to a time. You never see'd such a gletter in all your life. What colours, to be sure. Yaller and green and urd and blue, and all the most expensive silk and velvet. Zome o' the things was covered with jewels as big as yer thumb, and where 'twad'n jewels 'twas gold. They must have cost hunderds o' pounds.

'I don't zee how you'm gwain to get all that on,' I said to mother. 'You'll be the size of a houze.'

'Me?' her says. 'Most o' this is yours, stoobid.'

'Git out with 'ee, mine! What wude a man want with all that trumpery?'

'Git out yerzell. What wude a wumman want with two 'ats and two pair o' shoes.'

'Well,' I says, 'you ban't gwain to tell me that one o' they hats is a man's?'

'Coorse it is. That's yours.' Her held up a gaudy-lookin' thing, shaped like the spittoon in the parler turned up-an'-down.

'Rummage,' I said. 'You don't think I be gwain about with that thing on my haid, do 'ee?'

'I dunnaw where else you'd wear it. Cude'n be on yer veet, for certin.'

'But he've got a long feather in 'en.'

'What did 'ee want, then, a bunch o' carrots? Putt 'n on and let's see how you looks.'

'You don't want to putt 'n on to zee that,' I says. 'I shall look like a fule.'

And mother said, 'If it id'n gwain to alter 'ee no more than that I don't zee what you wants to grummle vor.'

Zo I putt the thing on, and you never zee'd such a sketch in your live. 'Gimme a stick and a couple strings of ing'ens,' I said, 'and I shall be complate.'

'You've got 'en on wrong, stoobid,' her saith. 'The feather shude be around one zide.'

'How do you knaw where the feather shude be?' I says. 'You never zee'd 'Enry Eight.'

'Don't be zo redecklus. What wude he want a feather sticked up in front vor?'

'To keep the flies off his nawse. I don't zee what gude else he is. Makes me look a gawk, eether-one o' the ways.'

'You can't expect no other without the rest o' the things. Slip on the coat and then zee. Better keep on the coat you've got, 'twill help full 'n out.'

He wanted a bit o' helpin', too. There was rume for me and another inzide thikky coat.

'I shall never come to it,' I said.

'Ees, you will,' says Ann, 'with a cushion or two.'

'Twas a hansum coat, sure nuff. Come right down to me knees he did, and he'd have stood upright by hiszell with the gold laace on 'en. There was nuff coloured glass about 'en to make a church winder, and around the neck was this-yer white fur with black spickets; what they calls vermin.

143

'That fur alone is worth a small fortune,' says Ann.

'So he might be, but 'tis gwain to be a darn nuisance ticklin' my yers.'

'Never mind about that,' says mother. 'Kings must get used to havin' their yers tickled.'

'I've got a-plenty rume to braithe, that's one thing,' I said.

'Us'll soon stap that, when us have stuffed 'ee out proper,' says mother; and I'm darned if her did'n spaik the truth that time. Jus' then Dicky Ozegude looked back to say he fergot to deliver the message that Squire and Mrs. Porter was gwain to look along about o' zix o'clock to finish us off and zee to my wiskers.

'What's wrong with my wiskers?' I said.

'I think Squire have got to titch 'em up a bit and make 'em look like 'Enry Eight.'

'Daun' he want to take the end off me nawse, and set me knees back a bit?'

'Be quiet, do', says Ann. 'You don't appreciate what anybody do's for 'ee.'

'It all depends what they do's,' I said.

'Us'll get dinner over quick,' her said, 'and then you'll have gude time to putt her things on and I can stuff 'em out as you goes.'

I shan't attemp' to discribe what I went droo thik arternune, but I tell 'ee straight I wished ole 'Enry Eight had never bin born. I managed the stockin's all right, after mother had poked in half the week's washin' to make the calves stick out behind; and then come the burches. They was tight as wax to the knees, but when come to the waist part I cude lop 'em over and the front part wude raiche around to the small o' me back. Mother reckoned her cude zoon putt that to-rights with a couple o' cushions, but it wad'n so aisy. I was fat nuff vore and back, if you understand, but too narrer to the zides. Mother said, 'You looks more like cabbical D than cabbical O.'

'I veels like sayin' a cabbical D?' I says, 'if that's aught to do wai 't.'

'No use you gettin' like that. All you wants is a piller each zide.'

Well, her putt a piller each zide, and then her had to tie 'em there with coords, 'cus they wude keep slippin' down. 'Genst her'd finished I lookid zac'ly like a viggy pudden in the clath, all ready to go in the pot.

'Look what you've done. I can't rest me arms down to me zides.'

'Nonsainse. That's your zides out there, not in where you thinks they be.'

144

Then her trigged me up in all the vinery, and hanged a golden chain about me nack, and sevver'l ribbins and things, and sticked the ole spittoon on me haid, and with the zame, in come Squire and Mrs. Porter.

Not that I shude 'a-knawed who 'twas if they had'n spoke. Squire was disguised to be a knight like you zees in the picsher bukes, with clothes all made o' tin, and a hoss's tail 'pon-tap of his hat. Soon's I started moanin' he said:

'You need'n grummle, Jan. I'm as bad off as ever you be. They've putt me in yer with the shoe-horn, and they'll have to get me out with the tin-opener.'

'I think Mr. Stewer looks lovely,' says Mrs. Porter. 'He'm 'Enry Eight to the very life.'

'I'd be glad if you cude tell me one thing, mam,' I said. 'How did 'Enry go on when he wanted to braithe?'

Caw! Did'n they laaf! 'There's one thing, Jan,' says Squire, "twill keep 'ee hot.'

'Hot, begad. I'm rinnin' down into straimes 'o sw'attin' now. What 'twill be like bim-bye I can't think.'

To make matters wiss, Squire had zome tacky ole trade and sticked hair all around my mouthe fer mustash and beard. Properly gubbed up I was with that muck, and made me veel as if me skeen was turned into brown paaper.

'What about Ann Bowling?' says Mrs. Porter. 'Come along, Mrs. Stewer. I'll help you dress.'

'I shan't take very long,' says mother. 'I don't make so much fuss as zome volks.'

'No,' I said, 'and you ab'm got to go about like a furniture removin' van.'

They dressed mother up and her come down so-proud as a paycock, and I must say her lookid very nice. Squire ordained takin' us over in his moter, but 'twas titch and go whether us wude all get in or no. You zee, Mrs. Porter was Quane 'Lizabeth, and her had one o' they dresses that sticks out all around like a wheatrick. Her and me had to go in behind. I was half-stood up all the way, and her had to turn around and kneel up top the sate. Nice way to take a king and quane about, I'm jiggered.

When us come to the plaace us had to walk up droo a long line of gappin' hobbidy-hoys, and the remarks they passed was most owdacious. Soon's I got out from the moter one aw'm olleyed out:

'Ullaw, Jumbo's come.'

'Giddout,' says another aw'm, 'that's the balloon. You'll zee 'en go up in a minute.'

'No 'tid'n, I know what 'tis. He've come to the wrong plaace. He thinks 'tis the fat baiste show.'

'Open the double doors there, Jimmy.'

That's the sort o' thing I had to putt up wai' all the way up droo, and when Quane 'Lizabeth passed along with her crinoline, zomebody said, 'How's the parrot gwain to manage till he gets back his cage?' Squire had it, too. When he appeared, one gawk holleyed out, 'Jimmy, one tin o' bully-bafe now comin' up.'

But when us got inzide, 'twas a wonderful zight, 'pon me word. There was scores there already, all dressed up in fancy rigs, and when you zee'd so many else makin' fules o' theirzel's you did'n mind lookin' daaft likewise; speshly as everybody had they black maskis on their faaces, so you cude'n own anybody. The dresses was all colours o' the rainbaw, and when the musickers striked up and the dancing beginned, 'twas a purty zight, begad.

But what I did suffer thik night for the Gude o' the Cause. I know that's what 'twas, 'cus every time I complained they said, 'Never mind, Jan, 'tis for the Gude o' the Cause.' I think I must have done the Cause a lot o' gude.

In the fus' plaace, I did think I was gwain to have a dance or two. Not that I knows very much about they new-fangled capers where you takes yer partner for a walk around the rume, but I reckoned I cude do it as well as zome aw'm. So me and mother stood up to it.

But, tell about dance! Why, I cude'n ketch her hold. Her was two cushions away, and the utmost I cude do was to putt the tips o' me vingers in under her arm-pits. You cude'n dance any sense like that. Us tried it for a bit, but 'twas a poor job. Us cude'n keep stap fer one thing. Furthermore, us occupied the space of two couples, and the rume bein' so full, it cude'n be spared. Every time us bumped into another couple mother wude be shoved right out o' my vingers. I'd have the works o' the world to get her again, 'cus the nex' couple wude come wizzin' into my front cushion and round I'd go, like a weather-cock; and bevore I cude right mezell, another lot wude give me a scat and send me spinnin' the oppozyte derection.

I tell 'ee, it id'n no aisy matter to guide two foot o' stummick in a rume full o'dancin' volks. I dersay 'Enry Eight cude manage it all right, 'cus he was brought up to it; but I don't think I cude have read the derections proper.

Then us tried it with mother comin' around one zide, where I was only one piller thick. That was a trifle better, but only what you might call for the Gude o' the Cause. One of us was boun' to go zideways, so us was everlastin' stappin' on each other's veet.

There's one thing, that did give me a chance to get zome o' me awn back, 'cus every time I come down all my weight 'pon mother's bes' corn, I told her 'twas for the Gude o' the Cause.

But wad'n I 'ot! I was never so 'ot in me life. What with they ole cushions, and the vermin round me neck, and jumpin' about tryin' to dance, and the rume like a oven, I was rinnin' down in straimes. And that made me start to tickle. My dear zaul, did'n I itch! But I cude'n scratch for cushions. And I reckon, when you'm itchin' dreadful and can't scratch the plaace you mus' be doin' the Cause a power o' Gude.

Mother was proper sorry for me, and done the best her cude, but I'll defy any other body to find the right spot, speshly amongs' a crowd o' volks. And I was itchin' a hunderd differ'nt plaaces to-once, mostly in under the cushions and pillers. I railly thought I must go mazed.

And then I had the wist misfortune o' the lot. The only way I cude get relief was to get up in zome corner o' the rume where volks wude'n notice me, and move the old cushions about. Sort of scratch mezelf with 'em. It must have looked funny to zee anybody pushin' their stommick round and round. But I'd got in that staate I did'n care what it looked like. 'Twas eether that or go out o' me mind.

But with workin' they pillers about so much I bust the coords that was keepin' 'em in plaace, and then I was properly done. I got one o' me stommicks around the zide in under my arm, and do what I wude I cude'n get 'n back. I was feared of me life to move. There I was forced to bide in one spot all they howers, 'cus if I dared to walk I shude have went I dunnaw what shape. So when they had the grand parade for the jidgin', Jan was missin'. Squire was turrable annoyed 'cus I wude'n join in.

'You'd almost sure to take fus' prize, Jan,' he said.

'I daun' want it, zur,' I answered 'en. 'I did'n come yer fer the prize; I come fer the Gude o' the Cause.'

So, as I zay, I'm gwain to have a Cause of my awn. I ab'm decided 'eet what it shall be. But it shall be a Gude Cause, I can assure 'ee o' that, and one which shall make everybody sit up that takes part in it. 'Twill make 'em look so redeclus, they'll be ashamed to zee theirzells; 'twill make 'em uncomferable till they can hardly live; they shall ache in every joint, and they shall itch in every spot where they can't reach to scratch. They shall be too 'ot to braithe, too fat to sit down, and too tired to stan' up; and to cap the lot they shall have to pay money for it.

Ees, I shall have a Gude Cause, that all the other volks with Causes o' their awn shall be frightened to come near me, 'feared I shall ketch 'em with mine. I'll larn the beggers, I will.

THE END

A complete list of Alan Sutton books,
including country titles
is available from:
Alan Sutton Publishing, Dept CB,
30 Brunswick Road, Gloucester, GL1 1JJ

POACHER'S PIE

FRED ARCHER

Poachers, princes and plum-pickers all have their say in this book by Fred Archer which celebrates the lives of the little master men who grew their asparagus and cabbages on the black soil of the Vale of Evesham. He writes of the market gardeners, upright and industrious, and of the men who worked for them, like Kick Pudding, the student of Darwin. And he tells of the farmers who considered themselves above cabbages, employed the farm labourers in their tied cottages, and hunted with the emigré French dukes. These Orleanist princes lived in great style just down the Worcester road at Wood Norton Hall, entertained the crowned heads of Europe to hunting and shooting and provided the folk of Evesham and Ashton with jobs, certainly, but also with an endless source of enjoyable and scandalous speculation in the Whistling Ploughman or the Jolly Gardeners.

The well-stocked coverts of Wood Norton also provided temptation and the killing of one of the Duke's keepers resulted in a murder trial at Worcester assizes in 1890. In the powerful centrepiece of his book, Fred Archer retells the whole stark story of the poacher brothers, Sam and Joe Boswell and their accomplice Lovely Hill, from the newspaper reports of the time and from the memories of people, including his own mother and uncle, who knew the families involved.

Poacher's Pie is a book of riches, teeming with people from every walk of life in Fred Archer's Cotswolds.

176pp   216mm × 135mm
ISBN 0 86299 428 4 (paper) £4.95

JUST AROUND THE CORNER

HUMPHREY PHELPS
With illustrations by Hugh Moss

Humphrey Phelps farms just over two hundred acres in west Gloucestershire. Both his father and grandfather farmed in the same district. He is married and has three sons.

He says he was not the small boy of his story and never had an Uncle George. However, he assures us he knew people just like the characters in *Just Around the Corner*. Sadly, they are disappearing, victims not so much of the passing years but of so-called 'Progress'.

Just Around the Corner records the sadness and the gaiety, the gravity and the humour of village life at the end of the 1930s as seen through the eyes of a mischievous, observant and essentially human small boy. The story leaves a satisfying and agreeable flavour in the mouth.

160pp   216mm × 135mm
ISBN 0 86299 443 8 (paper) £4.95

UNCLE GEORGE AND COMPANY

HUMPHREY PHELPS

Uncle George is back. That lovable old rogue who surfaced in Humphrey Phelp's previous stories of country and farming life. *Just Across The Fields, Just Over Yonder* and *Just Where We Belong*, now has a book all to himself.

Some time before the war Uncle George threatened to finish with baking – although, some say, the way he was running it in those last few years, it had almost finished with him too. He became a full-time smallholder, able to follow his natural bent and indulge in all his favourite pastimes.

A shed stood in the garden covered in honeysuckle and it was here that Uncle George pondered upon the strange ways of the world and men, and the stranger, unfathomable ways of women. (He was a bachelor and rather wary of women in general.) It was here also that he spent his time thinking of new schemes or even newer schemes when the earlier ones went awry as they sometimes did. And there are lots of schemes and adventures in this rollicking and affectionate portrait.

160pp   216mm × 135mm
ISBN 0 86299 444 6 (paper) £4.95